Walter Raleigh Vaughan

Vaughan's Freedmen's Pension Bill

Walter Raleigh Vaughan

Vaughan's Freedmen's Pension Bill

ISBN/EAN: 9783337411824

Printed in Europe, USA, Canada, Australia, Japan

Cover: Foto ©Andreas Hilbeck / pixelio.de

More available books at **www.hansebooks.com**

VAUGHAN'S

"FREEDMEN'S PENSION BILL."

BEING AN APPEAL IN BEHALF OF MEN
RELEASED FROM SLAVERY.

A PLEA FOR

AMERICAN FREEDMEN

AND

A RATIONAL PROPOSITION TO GRANT PENSIONS
TO PERSONS OF COLOR EMANCIPATED
FROM SLAVERY.

BY
WALTER R. VAUGHAN,
OMAHA, NEBRASKA.

DEDICATED TO

W. J. CONNELL, the brave representative in the halls of the American Congress, from Nebraska, who dared to say that the slave of a century is entitled to financial recognition because of former wrongs. To him it is dedicated by the author of this book and also the Pension Bill.

By his friend,

WALTER R. VAUGHAN.

SLAVES FROM 1620 TO 1862—242 YEARS—SANCTIONED BY THE UNITED STATES.

PREFACE.

In approaching a work that I deem to be of national importance, it may be a duty I owe to my countrymen, whether white or black, to say that I have been moved in the direction of asking the Government to provide pensions for former slaves by a sense of duty which I esteem the Government to owe to men who have been the unwilling subjects of lawful authority adversely to their natural right of personal liberty. The people made free by Presidential Proclamation, and confirmed in their freedom by amendments to the Federal Constitution, and by the organic laws of those States where slavery was a recognized institution prior to the war of the rebellion, have certain natural rights that neither the puffs of newspaper writers nor the whimsical cant of small fry politicians can oppress into obedient silence. The fact stands forth in historic writ that an enslaved black race has been set free after a lifetime of service to masters not of its own choosing. During the years of negro servitude colored men, women and children have been rated as chattels and taxed as such for the exclusive benefit of the white race. Courts, schools and benevolent institutions have been established and maintained upon the blood and sweat of the negro race. The cattle upon southern plantations returned less money into the public treasury for the maintenance of educational institutions than negro chattels held into slavery through a system of traditional wrong. The direct beneficiaries of the system of slavery were not responsible for a wrong entailed upon them. Until the way for emancipation was opened, by the circumstances of war, the freedom of the Africo-American race was nearly if not quite impracticable.

The vicissitude of civil war presented a gloomy picture in the history of the American republic. States dissevered, homes divided and old-time personal friends made public enemies, are but a few of the wretched features of the days made vivid by the continuous gun-powder flashes that burst upon the eyes of an amazed people from Bull Run to Appamattox—from 1861 to 1865. Amidst the din and clash of horrid war but one rainbow of heavenly promise beamed upon the American people as a result of the collapse of the Confederacy. A harbinger of good will came in the assured freedom of the previously condemned slave. Slowly from the ruin of war the States were rehabilitated, and took their places as members of the Constitutional Union. At every stage of reconstruction the freedom of the negro was made more certain, and in that work the doom of slavery was forever settled upon the North American continent.

But the freedom of the negro has not compensated the families turned adrift from home and bade to work for personal subsistence. In old age, and many in the throes of poverty, they appeal to the Government that made them free to furnish them a necessary support. The Government has no right to convert the circumstances of their freedom into a condition of absolute cruelty. If the saviors of a nation are entitled to the aid of the Government, surely the wards of the nation are worthy of practical assistance.

Be just to the blacks of the days of slavery. Their recognition as citizens, worthy of compensation for past errors of the Government, will do more to elevate the fame of a great nation that dares to be just, even at a late hour, than all the story of its brilliant achievements in arms. The glory of American freedom will be made perfect in the pension of the surviving slaves of the ante-bellum period.   WALTER R. VAUGHAN.

OMAHA, NEB., October 1, 1890.

VAUGHAN'S PLEA FOR THE OLD SLAVES.

The work of history, written in the interest of the races of mankind, has been sadly deficient in its efforts to do justice between the various elements of civilization. In surveying the field of universal population that spreads over a myriad of climes, making up a world, it must be apparent to the interested observer that the field of progress has been disputed from the beginning, only to be acquired in the end by those elements of nationality which secured domination here and there by means of force. The people who were subdued fell into despondency and at length into slavery.

It is not the purpose of the writer to delineate the advancement of the northern races that made progress in the work of civilization, or to decry the lassitude that enveloped the people of warmer climates who eventually became a prey to their more vigorous neighbors. The recognition of might in making right the will of those in power has done much in the direction of giving tyrants their sway, and of transmitting their authority to those who may arise in the line of heredity. Nations have been born and made to rule simply at the behest of adjacent power. Kings have advanced the rules of kingdoms by placing members of royal families in control of provinces conquered by the work of war.

In the advancement of power it has naturally followed that those who were weak fell into communities by themselves, and they became the prey of their more powerful neighbors. As far as they could they resisted predatory incursions designed to make vassals of captives; but the fact is indisputable that human slavery was born of captive people made prisoners from the circumstance of war.

Once the existence of human slavery had gained a foothold within the domain of a powerful monarch, it was an easy work for the navies of that monarch to spread the institution wherever there was a demand for labor. The slave trade sprang up and flourished at the will of potentates whose provinces were enrinched by the products of slave labor.

According to Chambers' Encyclopedia, which states the case very fairly, the negro slavery of modern times was a sequel to the

discovery of America. Before that discovery African negroes,
who were but races of savages, enslaved their captives taken in
war. That is to say, a successful tribe made slaves of its prisoners
taken from an unsuccessful or weaker tribe. The Arabs, who
were roving bands of merchantmen, made a regular trade in
negroes who were captives of warlike expeditions. After the discoveries of Columbus, and those who followed in his wake, the de-
portation of Africans to the plantations and mines of the New
World raised the value of captive negroes and gave to them a
market value. Instead of putting captives to death, as had been
the custom, thenceforward they were sold into slavery and shipped
to North or South America or to adjacent islands. The Portugese,
who possessed a large part of the African coast, began the work of
importing negro slaves to America, and other seafaring nations
quickly followed in the remunerative trade. England furnished
her quota of merchants and merchant ships to carry on a business
wherein traders made fortunes. No less than 300,000 slaves were
conveyed under the British flag from the coast of Africa between
the years 1680 and 1700, and between 1700 and 1786 the vast
number of 610,000 were exported from Africa to the Island of
Jamaica, a British province, to say nothing of the vast army
thrust upon the British colonial possessions of North America.

The British nation, that engaged so earnestly in the work of
planting slavery on the soil of the New World, took an early part
in suppressing the African slave trade and also in the work of emancipation. A society for the suppression of the slave trade was
organized in London in 1787. The parliamentary leader in this
great work of humanity was William Wilberforce, who occupied
about the same relation to the British parliament of a century ago
that William E. Gladstone does to the parliament of to-day. The
bill presented by Wilberforce, looking to the abolition of the
slave trade, failed in 1791, but under the leadership of Mr.
Fox it subsequently became a law and was made operative
after January 1, 1808. The United States followed Great
Britain in the suppression of the slave trade. Other countries
joined in suppressing the traffic. But Englishmen continued
the nefarious work for a number of years under the protection of
the flags of both Spain and Portugal. In 1811 the British parliament, under the leadership of Lord Brougham, made participation
in the slave trade a felony, and in 1824 it was declared piracy,
punishable with death.

But while this work of reform had been spreading over the world the slave traders of Great Britain had succeeded in planting the institution of slavery upon a firm basis in the British provinces of North America. Hence those colonies had been easily made the recipients of British rape upon the savage tribes along the coast of Africa. In this way American colonists, to whom large grants of land had been made in North America, became enriched without severe effort on the part of the grantees. English slavers poured a horde of African captives upon the American colonies and compelled planters to buy them as a condition of British protection. In 1618 the British ship Treasurer was engaged in the slave trade and landed African negroes from the mouth of the Congo river upon the banks of the James. The following year a Dutch man-of-war, sailing under commission of the Prince of Orange, landed upon the coast of Virginia a cargo of 14 negroes, and the next season a cargo of 39 souls was landed at Jamestown. These were placed on the market for sale, payable in tobacco, which seems at that time to have been the currency of the realm. An able-bodied African slave was sold for 60 pounds of tobacco, and the purchasing planter was supposed to have paid the full value of the poor negro's body and soul in the transfer.

It was, perhaps, forty years after the introduction of slavery into Virginia before the work of planting involuntary African servitude upon American soil was countenanced by acts of the Virginia colony. In 1662 an act was adopted in the Colonial Assembly of Virginia providing that slaves might be held as subjects of law. Previously to December 14, of that year, slavery existed without legal authority, but the sale of men and women, the separation of families and the helpless condition of children born in slavery induced a law regulating the sale of slaves; and perhaps that law remains unrepealed and in effective force to-day, save the fact that subsequent conditions may have annulled it.

An exhaustive examination fails to furnish any data going to show that Virginia as a state made any revocation of laws adopted in ante-revolutionary days establishing colonial slavery. It was natural that olden laws should be accepted as part of the first constitution of Virginia, under the federal system, and that slavery should have been recognized as a state institution.

The condition of African slavery existing in Virginia, in pursuance of colonial custom and law, naturally extended into the territorial dependencies of Virginia, and might have remained as an institution until emancipation came, but for the act of congress in 1787, which excluded slavery from the northwestern territory ceded by Virginia to the United States.

At the organization of the Federal Government the institution of slavery existed in all of the original thirteen states. It was not alone in the states south of Mason and Dixon's line that slavery was a fixed institution, but in the other commonwealths, which became partners of the South in resistance to the tyranny of King George, there were slaves held by the white inhabitants under authority of local law. By virtue of the first federal census, taken in pursuance of the constitution of the United States, and under the authority of George Washington, then serving the first presidential term of the new republic, we find the following slave population returned in 1790—just one hundred years ago:

Connecticut	2,759
Delaware	8,887
Georgia	29,264
Kentucky	11,830
Maryland	103,036
New Hampshire	158
New Jersey	11,423
New York	21,324
North Carolina	100,572
Pennsylvania	3,737
Rhode Island	952
South Carolina	107,094
Vermont	17
Virginia	293,427
Territory south of Ohio river	3,417
Total	697,897

It is thus made to appear that the people of the Federal States looked upon slavery as an established institution at the incipiency of our Government, to be regulated with respect to commerce abroad and domestic security at home. Two-thirds of a million of slave people were recognized as a part of the people of the Federal Government. From that day until the first proclamation of Abraham Lincoln, dated September 22, 1862, looking to the emancipation of the colored race from bondage, the existence of slavery as a national institution was recognized in law, and by the administration in power at the seat of the General Government as a fixed institution of the new republic. The Northern States, one after another, that looked upon the institution of slavery in 1790 as existing by recognition of the National Government, adopted acts of gradual emancipation which freed them from the stigma of slavery early in the nineteenth century. Yet it is a fact that slaves were held in several of the states north of Mason and Dixon's line as late as 1840.

The history of the warfare against slavery instituted by William Lloyd Garrison, Wendell Phillips, Gerritt Smith, Horace Greeley and others of the old-time Abolition leaders goes to show that they never contemplated the forcible abolition of slavery. They looked upon it as an institution fastened upon the people by ancient colonial law, and they hoped to secure emancipation by making the institution repulsive to those who held slaves, and to appeal to their sense of justice for the obliteration of the lines that held black men in servitude.

Even as late as August 22, 1862, when the war of the rebellion was in full blast, President Lincoln expressed himself to Horace Greeley in the following forcible terms:

My paramount object is to save the union and not either to save or destroy slavery. If I could save the union without freeing any slave I would do it; if I could save it by freeing all the slaves I would do it; and if I could do it by freeing some and leaving others alone I would also do that. What I do about slavery and the colored race I do because I believe it helps to save this union; and what I forbear to do, I forbear because I do not believe it would help to save the union.

It will thus be seen that by the strongest friends of the colored race the question involved in the war of the rebellion did not contemplate the release of the slave from the bondage of serfdom. The idea paramount in the minds of the great men of the early war period contemplated no freedom for the slave, but merely the making of him an instrument in the suppression of an armed rebellion and the salvation of a constitutional union of the states, without regard to the immediate effect which the saving of the union might have upon the status of the negro. All men in high places looked upon the negro as an unwilling factor in the government, forced upon the states by the ancient British rule; and in saving the institutions planted upon this hemisphere by the fathers of the republic the condition of the negro had no part or parcel in the consideration of the men who sustained Abraham Lincoln during the early days of the rebellion. The circumstances of emancipation were compelled by the circumstances of war.

It is known and admitted that President Lincoln had in contemplation, early in 1861, the appointment of Stephen A. Douglas to the command of the army of the United States. Mr. Douglas at that date was willing to have slavery extended into free territory in case it was the will of the people; which, how-

ever, he did not believe to prevail. But with his known and
declared sentiments, had he lived, Mr. Douglas would most likely
have been made commander of the union armies, and it is possible
that he might have been the first declarent of slavery emancipation
within the states. The circumstances of his surroundings would
probably have pointed to him the line of duty as it appeared to
Mr. Lincoln in the progress of a carnage which finally made an
enslaved race free.

The meager incidents in the career of African slavery already
mentioned are sufficient in themselves to demonstrate that slavery
was planted within the United States by force, and was continued
under authority of law until emancipation was promulgated as a
measure necessary to ensure the quelling of an armed rebellion.
Emancipation was not a voluntary tribute to freedom, but was
extorted by the circumstances of war, as a measure necessary to
overthrow the power of insurgents against constitutional government. The men in authority at the time civil war began to rage
had no idea of making use of the negro as an agent in conquering
the rebellion. When it became manifest that it was a necessity
to make use of all the means which God and nature had placed at
the disposal of duly constituted authority, in order that armed
resistance against the government might be suppressed, then, and
only then, was the president moved to make a proclamation of
freedom to southern slaves. The person is not living, white or
black, who will presume to assert that Abraham Lincoln was not a
man of large heart, humane impulses and an earnest friend of
liberty to all mankind. But as president of the republic he
esteemed it his first duty to save the life of a nation, the government whereof had been committed to his hands. Mr. Lincoln was
not alone in this view. Cabinet officers, members of both houses
of congress, military commanders in the field, and in truth nearly
all the inhabitants of the loyal states accepted the same line of
policy as the governing principle of the war into which the nation
had suddenly plunged

In the progress of the war it became the policy of the United
States Government to enlist the services of negro soldiers as an
element directly interested in measures which, in the end, led to
the freedom of an enslaved race. It is perhaps true that the Confederacy took the first step in the direction of employing colored
troops, and in this way set a wholesome example to the Federal
authorities. Whether the enlistment of colored troops for service
in the Southern army contemplated the freedom of such soldiers

does not certainly appear. Had such freedom been promised, it is possible that a formidable army of blacks might have been recruited for the army of the South. But that negro soldiers were employed is pretty well established. The Charleston Mercury noted, within a fortnight after the attack upon Fort Sumter had been made, that several companies of the Third and Fourth regiments of Georgia had marched for the theater of war in Virginia, and that accompanying them was one company of negro soldiers from Nashville, Tenn., which had offered its services to the Confederate States and had been accepted. In the early part of May, 1861, a citizens' committee of safety at Memphis took steps to authorize C. Deloach, D. R. Cook and William B. Greenlaw " to organize a volunteer company composed of our patriotic free men of color, of the city of Memphis, for the service of our common defense." It does not appear that negroes held as slaves were asked to join the enterprise. Later on, February 9, 1862, there was a grand military review held in the city of New Orleans at which, according to the Daily Picayune, there were included " companies of free colored men, all very well drilled and comfortably uniformed." It was further stated that these negro soldiers had supplied themselves with arms without regard to cost or trouble, unaided by the Confederate Government. On this occasion " a fine war flag " was presented to Captain Jordan of the colored troops, and in response to the presentation the colored commandant delivered " one of his most felicitous speeches." It was not stated whether the " fine war flag " was ornamented with the stars and bars or whether it was of some other design. It is also historically narrated that about February, 1862, able-bodied colored men—contrabands, so-called—were taken to Richmond, formed into regiments and armed for the defense of that city. It is also known that Gen. Mansfield Lovell and Gen. Ruggles, in command at New Orleans prior to the advance of Gen. Benjamin F. Butler upon that city, from the direction of the gulf, had in their command a regiment composed of fourteen hundred men of color.

The fact of the enlistment of colored soldiers in the service of the insurrectionary states very probably had its influence upon the authorities at Washington, inducing the acceptance of negro troops in the Union service. At the beginning Mr. Lincoln hesitated in respect to his duty in placing arms in the hands of negroes. Others doubted the prudence of such a step, and it was the logic of circumstances rather than of deliberate design which opened the way for the formation of negro regiments in support of the Union cause. In 1862 Secretary of War Cameron authorized Gen. W. T. Sherman to accept the services of "loyal persons" who desired to aid in the suppression of rebellion in the vicinity of Port Royal. Gen. David Hunter very soon succeeded Gen. Sherman, and he found the authority given his predecessor among the military papers upon the files of his office. Gen. Hunter interpreted the authority to accept the services of "loyal persons" in a liberal spirit, and thereupon proceeded to enroll a regiment of blacks, which he officered with white men of recognized military skill and ability. The arming of the slaves in South Carolina opened a new feature in the progress of the war and occasioned manifest surprise in the halls of congress. The Hon. Charles A. Wickliffe, of Kentucky, introduced in the house of representatives a resolution of inquiry respecting the action of Gen. Hunter, which called forth a formal correspondence between Edwin M. Stanton, the successor of Mr. Cameron in the War Department, and the Hon. Galusha A. Grow, then Speaker of the House. The conditions which prompted the course of Gen. Hunter were fully stated and the action of the General was fully approved. In regard to the effectiveness of the colored troops thus brought into the service of the Union army, Gen. Hunter spoke in the highest terms of praise. He said: "The experiment of arming the blacks, so far as I have made it, has been a complete and even a marvelous success. They are sober, docile, attentive and enthusiastic, displaying great natural capacities for acquiring the duties of the soldier. They are eager beyond all things to take the field and be led into action, and it is the unanimous opinion of the officers who have had charge of them that, in the peculiarities of this climate and country, they will prove invaluable auxiliaries, fully equal to the similar regiments so long and successfully used by the British authorities in the West India Islands." Gen. Hunter concluded his answer to Mr. Wickliffe's congressional resolution by saying that he hoped to be able to present to the Government from forty-eight to fifty thousand of hardy, devoted negro soldiers by the next autumn. This fondly expressed hope was not realized, but of the gallant black soldiers who did enlist under the banner of the Union there were none who failed to do valiant service for a restored Union and in the cause of the freedom of their race.

When Gen. Hunter's communication to Secretary Stanton was read before the House of Representatives, Congressman Dunlap offered a resolution of censure because of the sentiments expressed therein; but the resolution was not then acted upon, and reflection no doubt satisfied Mr. Dunlap of the unwisdom of his proposed censure. At least he did not again call the attention of the house to the subject. While the censure was not voted, the important facts narrated by the distinguished soldier began bearing fruit in an unexpected quarter. Two senators of the United States called upon President Lincoln and proffered to him the services of two fully equipped negro regiments, which the president did not feel authorized to have mustered into the union service. One senator allowed his angry passions to arise, and very impudently told Mr. Lincoln that he hoped to God he would resign from the chief magistracy and let some man succeed him who had a little backbone. The same senator was very glad to assent to the re-election of Abraham Lincoln two years later.

A careful survey of the difficulties that surrounded the introduction of the despised black man into the office of a soldier gives, even at this late day, some idea of the prejudices which had to be overcome in order to save the union of the states from threatened dissolution. Thousands were precipitate and impracticable, and other thousands were diffident and impracticable. But in the meantime the negro stood ready to do his part; and although some statesmen were doubtful and hesitating, and others importunate and exacting, the subjects of solicitude were preparing to strike for the perpetuity of the government of their devotion. A thousand enthusiastic lovers of their own race, as well as of the flag they had known as the emblem of freedom to the white race, stood banded together in pursuance of Gen. Hunter's recognition of their right of enlistment; and they succeeded in finding their way into the general military service under an emergency. Secretary Stanton wrote Gen. Saxton saying that "in view of your command and the inability of the government at the present time to increase it in order to guard the plantations and settlements from invasion, and to protect the inhabitants thereof from captivity and invasion by the enemy, you are authorized to arm, uniform and equip and receive into the service of the United States such number of volunteers of African descent as you may deem expedient, not exceeding five thousand," etc. That order enabled Gen. Saxton to get his waiting regiments into service. It enabled him to organize five other regiments. It deprived the rebellion of the direct support of the men who might otherwise have cultivated the fields and raised crops for the sustenance of southern armies. It opened a new field for the negro, and charged him with a grand importance in crippling the power of the white master, and enabling the black serf to do his part in bringing an armed rebellion to final confusion and ultimate defeat. President Lincoln withdrew reluctantly from the position he originally assumed in opposition to the equipment of negro troops, and finally gave countenance to orders issued from the war department authorizing the formation of negro regiments.

As a matter of history, it may be stated that before the date of accepting distinctive negro companies or regiments in the service of the union army, many colored men were enlisted in the service in their individual capacity, notably in eastern regiments. The state of Massachusetts, for instance, authorized such enlistments and received recruits from other states which were credited upon the quota of enlistments necessary to exempt the Old Bay State from the provisions of the draft laws enacted by congress. Colored volunteers were recruited in Indiana, and perhaps in many other states, and sent to Massachusetts in order that they might be mustered into the union service without objection being raised on account of color. It has never been learned that those soldiers failed to prove less efficient, resolute, brave and daring than the most courageous and valiant of the white enlisted men.

Throughout the south it was found that negroes flocked in numbers to union encampments, beyond the facilities of army officers to equip them for military service, as union troops advanced into the heart of the Confederacy. Those who had been reared in the extreme south, or in the very center of the cotton belt, manifested an intense desire to take up arms in behalf of the union cause far in excess of the colored element along the border and in proximity to the free states. It required months of war and excitement to instill into the minds of those negroes, far removed from contact with northern men and northern sentiment, the fact that a military revolution was in progress that must necessarily terminate in a marked change touching their political relations. Once convinced, however, of the truth, the negro proved to be an important and willing factor in bringing final success to the union cause.

As early as the month of June, 1862, negroes flocked to the encampment of Gen. Phelps, who had made his way into the rural regions of Louisiana. While resting from the fatigue of hurried marches and almost continual skirmish fighting, in the vicinity of Carrollton, the General found his camp crowded daily with fresh fugitives from the captivity of slavery. He could not support them in idleness, and a sense of the great work in hand forbade the return of the fugitives to the possession of masters from whom they had escaped. He therefore afforded protection to such as manifested a willingness to shoulder a musket and endure the vicissitude of war as a recompense for personal liberty. The condition of his surroundings was made known officially by Gen. French to Gen. Butler, who was then in command at New Orleans, and the propriety was suggested of recommending that the cadet graduates from West Point be sent into the South to organize and discipline negro levies, so as to make them efficient soldiers for use in the pending war. Very clearly Gen. Butler did not like the suggestion. He advised the employment of "contrabands," as he called them, for fatigue duty, but forbade their employment in the capacity of soldiers. In writing to Gen. Butler, under date of July 31, 1862, it will be found that Gen. Phelps said: "I am not willing to become the mere slave-driver you propose, having no qualifications that way." Thereupon he resigned his commission and backed out of the war.

It will be seen, in the circumstances just narrated, as well as in the diffidence of the president and others high in civil authority, that the ambition of the negro to fight for his freedom was handicapped at almost every point. When the slaves found that a vigorous prosecution of the war meant a speedy reduction of the revolted states to the recognition of a supreme American Union, under which the permanent freedom of their race would have ample guarantee, their anxiety to take a hand in the great fray was intensified in every quarter. Their appeals to do service forced a hearing in the halls of congress. The failure of the Army of the Potomac to capture Richmond, after seven days of blood-red carnage, no doubt had a tendency in the direction of inducing congress to make use of all the elements at command which seemed to promise a speedy peace. To this end the Hon. Henry Wilson, chairman of the senate committee on military affairs, introduced a bill, July 16, 1862, empowering the President to accept all persons of African descent, for the purpose of constructing intrenchments or performing camp service, or any war service for which they may be found competent! The peculiar phraseology of the Wilson bill gave color to the idea that, even as late as midsummer 1862, the ability of the negro to make a good soldier was seriously questioned by high authority in the senate of the United States. Most truly the willing and anxious man of color had a hard time

proving his right to fight the battles of his country in a war that
involved his own liberty and the freedom of all the people of
his race.

It was not until the winter of 1863 that official action was taken
authorizing the enlistment of distinctively negro regiments. An
order was issued by the secretary of war, January 26, 1863, authorizing Gov. Andrew, of Massachusetts, to raise two regiments
of negro troops to serve two years. Accordingly the Fifty-fourth
Massachusetts was organized and equipped, and was mustered into
the military service May 13, 1863, being the first complete regiment of negro troops called to duty in quelling the rebellion. It
was ordered to proceed to South Carolina, but so great was the
prejudice at the North against negro soldiers that the chief of
police in the city of New York informed the war department
that he feared the regiment would be subjected to insult in case it
passed through that metropolis. However, his fears appear to have
been groundless, as the regiment passed on its way rejoicing.
About the same time Adjutant General Thomas personally took
charge of the business of organizing negro regiments from among
the contraband negroes gathered at and near military encampments
along the lower Mississippi, and October 13, of the same year,
Gen. Thomas authorized his assistant, Gen. E. D. Townsend, to
issue a general order providing for the enlistment and equipment
of negro troops. This was the first general recognition of the
negroes to become soldiers of the republic at all times and in all
places where recruiting was carried forward; and the third article
of General Order No. 329 provided that "all persons enlisted into
the military service shall forever thereafter be free."

This was the first absolute proclamation of emancipation issued
in the great civil war. Following its promulgation the enlistment
of colored soldiers went forward with alacrity in every quarter.
Within sixty days 2,300 negro troops were enlisted in New York
city, and by December 4, 1863 (about fifty days after the issuance
of Gen. Thomas' order) three full regiments of regulars had been
mustered into the United States service at Camp William Penn
near Philadelphia. Subsequently six other regiments were
recruited at the same place. From all quarters reports of enlistments of colored troops go to show that fully one hundred
thousand men had responded to the call of the country by the
opening of the year 1864, and fully half that number had been
mustered into service. They stood with guns in their hands ready
to fight for freedom at the drop of a hat.

The history of the great civil war is rich in its testimony of the patriotism of the negro and his devotion to the union cause, after he had learned the real purpose of the struggle and the government had receded from its rigidity against the employment of colored troops for the suppression of the rebellion. The record made by the negroes entitles the race to grand recognition. By the time of Lee's surrender 186,017 had done honorable service in the union army. Of this number the New England states furnished 7,916 troops; the three states of New Jersey, New York and Pennsylvania furnished 13,922; the western states and territories furnished 12,711; and the southern states (including the District of Columbia, 3,269) furnished 108,755 good and true men. In this splendid record the army rolls record the fact that there were 13 colonels, 27 lieutenant-colonels, 42 majors, 256 captains, 292 first lieutenants and 479 second lieutenants. Evidently the negro got to the front as rapidly as circumstances afforded him an opportunity.

In stating the obstacles that stood in the way of the negro race being able to don the blue, and wear it with honor, no reflection has been made upon the Government, which was slow to accept the service of armed negroes as soldiers of the republic. The president and his advisors merely followed a line of policy that was co-eval with the existence of the republic. Mr. Lincoln did not wish to place the colored race in a difficult position. On the contrary his feeling was most kindly; but he found himself in an abnormal position. As the representative of an anti-slavery sentiment he was made president; but his election did not contemplate more than prudent measures to prevent the spread of the slave institution. The abolition of slavery by means of federal encroachment upon state authority was an idea that had never entered his mind, and he would have rejected the thought with indignation had it been suggested to him as a measure of policy or right. When the time for universal freedom came he was ready for the emergency, but he did not seek it. The war came on; Mr. Lincoln accepted the negro as an element that might be instrumental in the salvation of the Union, and his confidence was not misplaced. Over nearly incomprehensible objections the negro became a soldier while the war was yet raging between the North and South. Now look to the record he made as a soldier.

The first black regiment enlisted for the war was the First South Carolina, commanded by Col. Higginson. Its first material service was an expedition to the St. John's River country, in

Florida, where it was met by sturdy resistance from southern troops, intensified by a natural repugnance of southern white men against confronting negroes with arms in hands. In all its skirmishes the South Carolina troops met with good success. In recounting the results of his expedition the Colonel commanding said in every instance his troops came off with unblemished honor and undisputed triumph, and the men had even appealed to him for permission to pursue the flying enemy. His colored troops were brave even unto a fault. No wanton destruction was permitted, and no outrages occurred during the expedition. In his official report Col. Higginson said: "No officer of the regiment now doubts that the successful prosecution of the war now lies in the unlimited employment of black troops."

At the investment of Port Hudson, in May, 1863; the First Louisiana regiment, organized at New Orleans, under the direction of Gen. Butler, was given a prominent position. Col. Stafford addressed the troops saying: "Protect, defend, die for, but do not surrender the regimental flag." The color-bearer, Sergeant Planciancois, responded: "Colonel, I will bring these colors back to you in honor, or report to God the reason why." When asked if he could take a certain battery in an engagement of the war of 1812, a brave American officer modestly replied, "I will try, sir," and he took it. His historic words were not more brave than those of Sergeant Planciancois at the siege of Port Hudson.

In the official report of the reduction of Port Hudson General Banks said: "On the extreme right I posted the First and Third regiments of negro troops. The First regiment of Louisiana engineers composed exclusively of colored men, excepting the officers, was also engaged in the operations of the day. The position occupied by these troops was one of importance, and called for the utmost steadiness and bravery in those to whom it was confided. It gives me pleasure to report that they answered every expectation. Their conduct was heroic. No troops could be more determined or more daring. They made, during the day, three charges upon the batteries of the enemy, suffering very heavy losses, and holding their position at nightfall with the other troops on the right of our line. The highest commendation is bestowed upon them by all the officers in command on the right. Whatever doubt may have existed before as to the efficiency of organizations of this character, the history of this day proves conclusively to those who were in a condition to observe the conduct of these regiments, that the government will find in this

class of troops effective supporters and defenders. The severe
test to which they were subjected, and the determined manner in
which they encountered the enemy, leave upon my mind no doubt
of their ultimate success. They require only good officers,
commands of limited numbers, and careful discipline, to make
them excellent soldiers." On the strength of the charges of the
negro soldiers at Port Hudson upon confederate batteries, George
H. Baker wrote and published a poem after the style of "The
Charge of the Six Hundred," which fully rivals that noble pro-
duction in excellency.

At the Battle of Milliken's Bend, June 6, 1863, 3,000
confederates attacked the command of Gen. Dennis, composed
in the main of about 1,250 black troops. The latter held their
ground, and such was their heroism in action that their gallantry
excited general commendation in union circles. Gentlemen
connected with the Confederate service freely acknowledged that
negroes, armed with death dealing weapons and led by experienced commanders, constituted a soldiery that would challenge
the admiration of the world.

Along the coast of South Carolina, and to the southward, the
naval victories of the union forces were aided in accomplishment
by negroes, and might have been impossible but for the brave
work of enlisted men of color who there made a record which has
become imperishable. The soldiers who figured in these engagements were enlisted, in a large measure, pursuant to the directions
of Governor Andrew, of Massachusetts, and direct communication
was made with the Governor touching the bravery of the troops
he had put in the field in his capacity as governor of the state.
It may be truly said that all official reports on record, of those
engagements wherein negro soldiers participated, that a perfection
of gallantry has been awarded to black soldiers who took up arms
in the deep hour of their country's distress.

Following the recognized success of the government in making
perfect soldiers of men relieved from the bond of slavery, and of
other colored men who had borne arms in the department of the
south and in the region of country contiguous to the lower Mississippi river, the enlistment of colored troops was accepted as the
policy of the government in other fields of the great war. They
participated in the later engagements of the Army of the Potomac,
and largely composed the forces of Gen. Wild, who achieved a
substantial success over Gen. Fitzhugh Lee in the battle of Wilson's wharf. From the date of the introduction of colored soldiers

in the Army of the Potomac all opposition to the participation of such troops in the war subsided, and they were welcomed in all departments alike by officers in command and by their white comrades in arms. In his official report of the engagement at Nashville, Gen. James B. Steedman said that fully twenty-five per cent. of the union losses were suffered by colored troops. He placed upon record the declaration that he was unable to discover that color made any difference in the fighting capacity of the troops under his command. He remarked that white and black nobly did their duty as soldiers, evincing alike cheerfulness and resolution in the discharge of duty. The antipathy of white soldiers against their black comrades in arms appears to have subsided under the pressure of mutual dangers and their joint struggles for the success of the union cause.

The troops commanded by Gen. Birney in the East were largely made up of colored enlistments, and no part of the army made a better record for gallantry or soldierly conduct. Gen. Lorenzo Thomas gave cheerful evidence to the fact that in the western armies most heroic service was performed by enlisted blacks at Paducah and Columbus, Ky.; at Memphis, Tenn.; at Vicksburg and Natchez, Miss.; at the works around New Orleans; at the Bridge of Moscow on the Memphis and Corinth line of railway, and at the investment of Fort Pillow, where colored men were babtized unto freedom in rivers of blood.

It is unnecessary to make special mention of the barbarity of the massacre of colored men at Fort Pillow further than to say that it has been condemned by the sense of the civilized world. It was inhuman in the highest degree. Gen. Chalmers, who was directly responsible for the butchery, appears to have been forgiven for his merciless order of "no quarter" by the black people of the south, inasmuch as thousands of them have repeatedly voted for his election to congress since the era of reconstruction; but there does not appear to have been unanimity among the colored voters in this respect, for the savage general has been regularly defeated at the polls in recent years.

It is unnecessary to follow the colored citizen of the United States further than has been done in the preceding pages with a view of according to him gallantry in arms. The sentiment of the American people has, long ago, settled in the line of admission that the negro was a brave, cool and disciplined soldier in all theaters of the great civil war wherein he had been afforded a fair opportunity for the development of his powers.

In civil life he has shown his capacity for self-government. In the senate of the United States II. R. Revels and Blanche K. Bruce, both of Mississippi, have given a good reputation to the colored people for a high order of ability. The same may be said of Jere Haralson and J. T. Rapier, of Alabama; J. F. Long, of Georgia; C. E. Nash, of Louisiana; J. R. Lynch, of Mississippi; B. S. Turner, of North Carolina; R. H. Cain, R. C. DeLarge, R. B. Elliott, Joseph H. Rainey, A. J. Ransier and Robert Smalls, of South Carolina; and J. T. Walls, of Virginia, all of whom have appeared in past years upon the floor of the house of representatives. Among the able diplomats who have reflected credit upon the American name abroad may be named Dr. Henry Highland Garnett, Prof. J. Milton Turner, Ebenezer D. Bassett, John M. Langston (now in congress), John H. Smith, and the world renowned Frederick Douglass. In the affairs of their respective states a large number of the colored men have done the people good service as members of the state legislatures, north and south, and in many local positions. Prominent among the last named class may be mentioned Sidney B. Hinton, of Indiana, who was elected to the office of Canal Commissioner by the general assembly in 1873, and afterwards became a member of the house of representatives from the capitol city and county of that state. When Mr. Hinton was elected to the office of canal commissioner one of his confreres upon the canal board was Thomas Dowling, a gentleman of wealth and distinction, whose personal record had encompassed a generous portion of the early history of the Hoosier commonwealth. Being approached by a small-fry politician, whose aim was to badger Mr. Dowling upon the contingency that required him to recognize a colored man as his political equal, the diminutive politician said:

"I congratulate you, Col. Dowling, upon being obliged to sit upon the canal board as the co-partner of Sid Hinton. How do you like a seat by a nigger anyhow ?"

Col. Dowling instantly replied: "I feel complimented, sir. I have known Mr. Hinton for twenty years, and I am honored in being placed at his side above what I would have been had you been elected canal commissioner instead of him. While he has devoted his time, talents and money towards the elevation of his race you have done your utmost to drag your race down."

This interesting dialogue at once came to a conclusion, and Col. Tom Dowling was not again molested with an insinuation that he had been obliged to recognize the political equality of a "nigger." Indeed it may be said that similar reflections upon the propriety of complete justice being done to the African race speedily died out when it became known that the negro was doing his utmost to merit the boon of freedom with which he had suddenly become clothed.

Even after more than a quarter of a century of freedom bestowed upon the men and women who were released from slavery by the direful arbitrament of arms, there is an influential and educated class of well meaning people who seem to doubt the capacity of the negro for self government. If such a doubt can rightfully exist, it only furnishes the most forcible reason that can possibly be assigned, why the general government and the state governments should exert every effort at the command of the people, to remove such a frightful disqualification from a mass of citizens in whose hands the ballot has been placed by the authority of the Federal Constitution. A free government can only be maintained upon a basis of general intelligence. The federal census, now being compiled, will probably show that the negro population of the United States amounts to one-ninth of the entire inhabitancy of all the states and territories. The black race is increasing in numbers more rapidly, in relative strength in this country, than the white race. With these facts confronting us it may be well to ask whether extraordinary measures are not absolutely demanded, looking to the lifting up in the scale of intelligence of a people who must continue to be a powerful fraction of our people for generations to come. Give to these men absolute justice. Pay them a stipend of their earnings during the years of their involuntary service. Place before them the means of bettering their condition. When released from penury they will be willing to accept a higher life, and to do their part in sustaining a government that has been just and fair to them. Give to them a measure of pension which is their national right.

During the present year a deliberative body known as the "First Mohonk Conference on the Negro Question," assembled at Lake Mohonk and engaged in a solemn discussion of the negro problem. It was accorded to the negro, by all participants in debate, that he was no weakling, and that his future must be determined in a sense of strict justice. One of the orators, Rev. A. D. Mayo, while assenting to the proposition that the negro was radical in his views, went on to say that he was also a very politic member of the community, in the endurance of that which he could not overcome, and in his tactful and even crafty appropriation of all opportunities. He has, as the reverend gentleman freely admitted, pushed in at every open door, listened while attending at the white man's table, hung about the church and huskings, taken in the celebration of the public occasion, and he has observed methods on election day even when he could not vote. He has been all eyes and ears, and even the pores of his skin have been open to the incoming of a practical education in life. Deprived, in a large measure, of the use of books, because of his inability to absorb their contents, and not possessing the ordinary apparatus of instruction, he has eagerly applied the circumstances of actual life, as it has come before him, to the betterment of his own condition ; and in very many respects he has made the application much more successfully than many of the " superior race " who have not been obliged to contend with a life of servitude in their struggle for existence. The negro has been called a creature of imitation. All men are such, in a certain degree, but it must be admitted that in the case of the blackman his imitations have been vastly helpful to his personal condition.

As the years pass by the resident negroes of the South, who were once slaves, will naturally become land-owners and the holders in fee of the homesteads whereon they reside. Many of them will become men of wealth as some have already done. The succeeding pages of this volume will indicate a few of many instances wherein the negro has raised himself from the cabin of slave days to opulence and high influence in church, school and state. As a class the southern negroes have no more idea of going to Africa than they have of undertaking a journey to the moon. Neither will they generally colonize into black communities, separate and apart from the white people. They are inhabitants of the republic, and by reason of habit and inclination they will remain in the land that has given them birth, and where home scenes and customs attach them to their surroundings. It is a part of the duty which society owes to them that they should be liberally assisted in making their conditions harmonious and conducive to the general welfare.

The conference at Lake Mohonk might have done a great deal for the weal of the negro, and incidentally for the welfare of society, had the delegates discussed, in a calm and dispassionate manner, the propriety of giving to the emancipated slaves a pension out of the plethoric treasury of the government. A discussion of means designed to benefit this class will find a responsive echo in the breasts of the black people beyond any high-flown resolutions respecting their moral condition or the supply of tracts and printed arguments upon abstruse questions. As the Lake Mohonk conference appears to be a permanent assembly, intended to have its annual meetings, it is very respectfully suggested that the next convocation shall devote its time to the discussion of practical questions.

In his line of discourse Dr. Mayo justly remarked that the old slaves were Southerners in their feelings and instincts. They were nearly unanimous in their devotion to the union cause in a time of war, and are so yet. They always will be. But in this respect they do not differ from the white people of the South, in the present day, for the union sentiment is now universal. But the negroes are Southerners, just as the residents of Massachusetts or Connecticut are New Englanders or the inhabitants of Nebraska are western people. As the political issues of the past fade into the distance the negro race will, more and more, act in all public affairs with the leading race with whom their companionship and direct interest belong. With proper encouragement and education the man emancipated from slavery will rise to his proper place in our great American family. But let the nation be just to him as it has been just to the soldiers of the union.

It is undeniable that the northern people who have organized societies and collected contributions for the betterment of the condition of the southern negroes, have looked to the enlargement of the religious elements, to which the contributors were denominationally attached, rather than to the elevation of the negro as a man. The negro does not require aid in order that the Methodist church, the Baptist church or any other church may be made numerically strong. He simply stands before the country as a petitioner for justice. Against the law of God and of humanity he has been held in bondage, and a great civil commotion has made him a free man. He is willing to accept all the agencies that the churches may organize for his spiritual advancement, and, as far as his innate piety goes, to extend thanks to the Almighty for a safe guide unto a better life. But at the same time he stands as a suppliant for justice. Over the pages of more than three centuries of American history there has been written the curse of slavery, of which the black man was the cruel victim. His servitude begot that degree of watchful care which is inseparable from self-interest. When the slave was sick he was provided with medical attendance; when he was hungry he was fed; when his clothes became threadbare, new habits were provided; when the continual strain of drudgery became irksome and detrimental a holiday was given with all the enlivening appendages of jollity and abundant humor. In a word the interest of the master required the creature comfort of his slave to be considered as a matter of prime importance. With emancipation the master's care of self-interest ceased. The government righted a great wrong by turning out the old slave to starve and die!

Instead of devising ways and means to secure the negro in his political rights, if these have ever been invaded, let the government of the United States take steps to habilitate the ex-slave with a sense of personal right which naturally attaches to his condition as a freeman, and to do that a reasonable recompense for the years of toil he suffered as a slave will be an act that will cast off much of this memory of his wrongs and will prove an incentive to the exercise of the duties and responsibilities devolving upon manhood. The man who feels that his government has been just to him is not likely to be inactive when the government points to an honorable service which he can perform in his capacity as a citizen for the honor of his country. Instead of quarreling and wrangling when he approaches the polls to deposit his ballot he will go as an orderly citizen, meeting political friends and antagonists with equal composure and confidence, and with a heartfelt prayer that the best cause may win. It is injustice that breeds bad feeling. A proper recognition of the claims of former slaves for pension by the government will obliterate the last trace of enmity that has resulted from our sad civil commotion and terrible appeal to arms. The north and the south will be a unit again.

In this hastily prepared sketch it has been imperfectly shown that negro slavery was planted upon American soil before the colonies had dissolved their dependency upon the British government. It has been shown that the parent government made the institution of slavery a fixture against the wishes of the people of the colonies. It has been sought to be established that the negro, in the days of slavery, was generally a tractable and obedient subject of his lawfully constituted masters. It has been set forth that, when the horrors of civil war began, a very large proportion of the negro slaves of the South felt disposed to espouse the cause of their masters, and many of them voluntarily engaged in acts of war in support of the rebellion. It has been the aim to make manifest the fact that when the black people became

thoroughly apprised that the advance of the union armies carried
with it freedom to the slaves they fell into a support of the union
cause with enthusiasm and stood ready to shed their blood under
the stars and stripes.   It has been made plain that the government
was slow to accept the service of black men as soldiers of the
republic, but that they proved themselves equal to the occasion
whenever they were allowed to do service, under arms, in their
country's cause.   It has been proven that many of the race have
demonstrated a high order of ability, and that they have made a
worthy record in Congress and in the diplomatic and consular
service of the government.

What the negro now requires is that kind of recognition which
will give him an independence begotten of his former condition as
a slave, wherein he performed his part nobly and well, so that his
freedom may prove a blessing to future generations instead of an
absolute curse.   It is not questioned that great encouragement has
been given negroes in providing means for their education and
placing them in an attitude to assert their rights and do their duty
as freemen.   But this service to men made free under such circumstances as surrounded the emancipation of Southern slaves falls far
short of a just recompense to men who suffered generations of
servitude in consequence of no sin of their own commission.   No
act that can now be done will place the old slaves and their
descendants in an attitude of equality, before the law, with those
white men of the nation to whom the laws once gave the fruits of
negro labor and the benefit of negro lives of unrecompensed toil.

It is respectfully submitted to the law-makers of the land that
the hour has arrived when the men and women who have been set
free without support, and without capital necessary to acquire
such support, ought to be cared for.   In the name of freedom,
thousands, yea millions, were turned away from comfortable homes
and sent adrift to provide for themselves.   In how many instances
were they old and poor ?   In their humble homes they said, one
to another, when they found the blessing of freedom to be a pos-
sibility for them and their children, "it surely must be the work of
the Lord," and on bended knees many a devout heart prayed
earnestly for deliverance.   Those same pious souls, when deliverance actually came, returned thanks to heaven for the sense of
liberty that pervaded the land and gave assurance to their own
hearts that they were free men and women.   They asked nothing
more of their country in that day than the privilege of eating the
bread that supported life with a perfect knowledge that it was

their very own, earned by toil to the fruits whereof no person
other than themselves could make a lawful claim. Such a thought
was a new sensibility to a people whose lives had been in ceaseless
subjection to a master's rule, and they were quite willing to take
up the burden of life without a complaint that they had no facilities in their new relations for the making of life enjoyable, or even
tolerable. But because they accepted freedom with light hearts it
cannot be said that the duty the government owes to its wards is
any the less sacred, and certainly that duty is not less obligatory
after the lapse of a generation in consequence of the long and
cruel delay.

The theory is tenable, and will scarcely be questioned, that
emancipation resulted as a military necessity rather than as a
political or social benefit conferred upon the recipients as a measure of justice and humanity. The slavery to which the negro was
subject in ante-bellum days was hereditary, and founded in ancient
error of government. But when that same negro became a nomi-
nal freeman without provision being made for him to engage in
the battle of life on a footing approaching something like equality
with others who sell their labor in the general market, in order
that they may acquire daily maintenance and reasonable independence, it must be apparent that he would suffer in the unequal
contest. He has been kept in a condition of vassalage but little
removed from the bondage formerly endured. He has been made
the prey of many heartless employers, because of his ignorance of
business methods, and of myriads of designing politicians because
of his insufficient knowledge of political economy. Give him the
means of reasonable independence and half the evils that surround
his present condition will be removed. In the bestowment of such
a gift the government will only discharge a part of the obligation
it owes for having made the negro a subject of taxation, like the
beasts of the field, during his years of involuntary servitude.

Since the day of the surrender of Gen. Robert E. Lee at
Appomattox, and the consequent knowledge that the freedom of
negroes held in slavery before the war was assured by the failure
of the Confederate States to maintain their existence as a united
government, the question "What duty does the United States
owe to the emancipated slaves?" has received much thought and
study on the part of the writer. Thoroughly impressed with the
idea that the changed condition of freedmen demanded the protect-
ing care of the federal government, it was a source of information
to confer with men occupying eminent station in political affairs.

in conversation and by personal correspondence, so as to gather their views on this essential point. Aside from personal interviews a great many statesmen were addressed by letter. Very little satisfaction was imparted by those who were addressed in their replies. In order to make this matter plain the following correspondence is inserted:

HIS FIRST THOUGHTS IN THEIR BEHALF TWENTY YEARS AGO.

In 1870, W. R. Vaughan, then a resident of Council Bluffs, Iowa, was called to Selma, Ala., his former home, to see his sick father, a farmer residing near that city, and while passing through Mississippi he wrote his wife the following letter:

On the cars in Mississippi, July 10th, 1870.

Mrs. Walter R. Vaughan, Council Bluffs, Iowa.

MY DEAR WIFE:—I am quite tired and it is very hot and dusty riding. I want to see you and our baby boy Walter very much. Will write you a long letter from Selma, Ala. Our cars are filled with former Mississippi slaves. Some have a few dimes to pay fare to the next station, others are forced to beg car fare. But few of them are half dressed. The government should pension these ex-slaves if they would right a great wrong. They formerly had good homes, were well fed, were provided with the best medical attention in sickness, and since their freedom just the reverse has been their portion. I do feel so sorry for the poor unfortunate creatures. I shall feel guilty, as an American, to the crime of enslaving them, until the government has paid them the debt justly due. I will be in Selma at 10 a. m. to-morrow. Write.

Affectionately your husband,

WALTER R. VAUGHAN.

LETTER OF APPEAL.

Council Bluffs, Ia., July 10, 1883.

DEAR SIR: The condition of persons who were once slaves, but were made free by the proclamations of Abraham Lincoln during the late war, and by the reconstruction of the civil governments of the states recently in rebellion, has suggested to my mind that something more should be done for those freedmen than merely declaring their personal liberty. Thousands of them have gone forth from homes of comparative comfort into circumstances of absolute penury. Of course the general declaration of freedom could not be hampered with the widespread conditions of individuals who came within the perview of Mr. Lincoln's proclamation, and hence an unconditional order of emancipation was a necessity and an act of right.

It has occurred to me that the proper thing for the government to do in the premises would be the placing of all ex-slaves upon a civil pension list in a sum sufficient to enable them to live without fear of certain want in their old age. The government has suffered them to be taxed as chattles since its organization, and as such they have contributed directly to the public support. To right a great wrong the government can do no better, it seems to me, than to make them pensioners for the residue of their existence, especially the aged and dependent.

I should be glad to learn your sentiments touching the propriety of the course proposed to be pursued, with any suggestion you may see fit to make in the premises. I have in view an elaborate discussion of the subject in a pamphlet or book. An early reply hereto will greatly oblige,

Yours very truly,

WALTER R. VAUGHAN.

Among others to whom the foregoing letter was addressed, it was mailed to the Hon. Benjamin Harrison, then a senator from the state of Indiana and now president of the United States. After a delay of something more than a month, the senator wrote as follows from his home in Indianapolis:

(See fac-simile letter on following page.)

United States Senate.

Ind'pls Ind.
~~Washington, D.C.,~~ Aug 17 1883

W. R. Vaughn Esq.
Council Bluffs Iowa

Dear Sir: Your letter in
relation to the subject of the
wrongs of Colored people and
your proposition for national
aid for them has been re-
ceived. I have not time to
make any contribution to
the discussion of this subject
myself. I will say, however,
~~that~~ I think the most
efficient way in which
the Government can aid
the Colored People is by some
provision ~~for~~ in ~~the~~ aid of
~~education~~ education in the
South.

Yours truly
Benj Harrison

It can scarcely be said that Gen. Harrison touched the point at issue. Still his suggestion of educating the freedmen manifested a knowledge of their dependent condition. Unfortunately the major part of the race were much too far advanced in life to become the subjects of school-boy instruction. For the younger ones most of the states have liberally provided school facilities, and it is a pleasure to know that in the main the colored people of the southern states, of the present generation, have enjoyed fair benefits of education.

A letter similar to the above, perhaps an exact copy, was mailed to Senator Preston B. Plumb, of Kansas. That gentleman furnished the following letter in reply:

FAC-SIMILE OF SENATOR PLUMB'S REPLY.

United States Senate,

Emporia, K., Aug 27

W. R. Vaughan, Eq
Council Bluffs, Iowa —
Dear Sir — I am in receipt of
your favor of recent date. Am
not quite prepared to agree
to the pensioning of able bodied
people, who are quite capable
of making a living — at least
until the Gov't has fully taken
care of its disabled soldiers.
Whether the bringing of Africans
to America was an advantage
or a disadvantage is one of the
questions about which we
differ & which is quite apart

[handwritten letter, partially legible]

from the iniquity of the system under
which they were captured & held
in bondage. It is not necessary
to enter upon this as I expect
no expansion — but that
you will see that if all Gov'ts
a to be held responsible
for all damages resulting
from the passage & execution of
laws, the unfortunate tax-payer
would be constrained bleed
out.

Wishing you success in your
undertaking

Respectfully yours,

[signature]

  The suggestion made by Senator Plumb that before any steps
shall be taken to provide pensions for "able-bodied people, who
are quite capable of making a living," it is the duty of the government first to take care of its disabled soldiers, is scarcely perti-
nent to the question under discussion. But as the soldiers have
been well provided with pensions, especially the unfortunate class
who suffered disabilities, there can be no room on that score for
withholding from the men who endured years of slavery, without
just cause, a recompense for the injustice they suffered for so many
years. The further remark of the senator, that "if all governments are to be held responsible for all damages resulting from the
passage and execution of laws, the unfortunate tax-payer would

be constrained to sell out,'' can scarcely have been well considered by him. The laws by which a race of people were enslaved for hundreds of years certainly do not have a place by the side of statutes that have occasioned trivial injuries or losses. Besides, for inconsiderable personal injuries the courts have commonly found means of redress, and the losses suffered have been adjusted in countless instances. For the flagrant wrong of slavery the victims have not been paid one cent.

Another senator whose opinion was sought was the Hon. O. H. Platt, of Connecticut. In answer Senator Platt wrote as follows:.

FAC-SIMILE OF SENATOR PLATT'S LETTER.

Long Lake N Y
Aug 25 1883

Hon W. R Vaughn

My dear sir

Your favor of recent date has been forwarded me to this place where I am spending a vacation You must Excuse me from writing any thing for publication upon the subject to which you allude. - I cannot see why the slaves now free, should be pensioned by the government, but shall read your work if I have the opportunity with interest

Very truly yours O H Platt

It will be plainly seen that neither of the gentlemen, the fac-simile of whose letters are given to the public in this volume, appear to have entertained a high admiration for the proposition to pension the ex-slaves. The tenor of their brief comments may properly be interpreted to be adverse to that proposition. Whether the advance of years may have affected an advance in the liberality and justice of their ideas remains to be seen, as they are all in high political station and may have a voice in the settlement of the question now formally submitted to an honest people through their representatives in the law-making branch of the federal government.

Fully seven years having passed away since this great subject was brought to the attention of members of congress, and others eminent in public life, the writer was forced to the conclusion that the only way left open for him to pursue was to prepare a bill setting forth the general purpose sought to be accomplished, and to procure its formal introduction into congress, in case a senator or representative could be found willing to have his name con-nected with a just measure having in contemplation a small per-centage of the compensation due from a great nation to a part of the human race it had held in slavery by the power of its gov-ernment, exercised in the enforcement of oppressive laws.

In conversation with the Hon. William J. Connell, representa-tive in the Fifty-first congress from the First District of Nebraska, that gentleman expressed his willingness to introduce the required bill and to take care of all correspondence that might come in his hands in consequence of such introduction. The writer esteems himself fortunate in having secured the help of Congressman Connell, which was accorded cheerfully. It is a pleasure to be able to say that Mr. Connell belongs to that class of public men who appreciate their relation to their constituents and who fulfill every respectable service required at their hands with assiduity if not real pleasure. In this instance the writer is happy in the belief that Mr. Connell is in full sympathy with the spirit of the measure he has laid before the house of representatives, and will do all that lies in his power to secure for it a fair consideration.

The bill presented by Mr. Connell was drafted by the writer (W. R. Vaughan, editor of the Omaha Daily Democrat and president of the Democrat Publishing Company), and the full text of the measure is as follows:

A BILL for an Act to provide pensions for freedmen released from involuntary servitude, and to afford aid and assistance for certain persons released, that they may be maintained in old age.

Prepared by W. R. Vaughan of Omaha, and introduced by Hon. W. J. Connell, M. C. from the First Nebraska District, by request.

Be it enacted by the Senate and House of Representatives of the United States, in Congress assembled:

SECTION 1. That all persons released from involuntary servitude, commonly called slaves, in pursuance of the proclamation of ex-president Abraham Lincoln, dated respectively September 22, 1862, and January 1, 1863, and in pursuance of amendments to the constitutions of the several states wherein slavery or involuntary servitude formerly existed, recognized by the federal constitution and laws of the United States, or by any law, proclamation, decree or device whereby persons once held as slaves or involuntary subjects, in consequence of race or color, or federal or state recognition of involuntary servitude, except for the commission of crime, whereof the party shall have been duly convicted, shall be and hereby are made pensioners upon the bounty of the United States, and also such persons as may be charged by laws of consanguinity with the maintenance and support of freedmen who are unable by reason of age or disease to maintain themselves.

SEC. 2. Any person who may have been held as a slave or involuntary servant under and by reason of any law of the United States, or in consequence of any device or custom prevailing within such states or the United States, except for the commission of crime whereof the party shall have been duly convicted, and who shall have been released from such servitude in manner before stated, and who shall at the date of the passage of this act have reached the age of seventy years shall be entitled to and receive the sum of $500 from the treasury of the United States, hereby authorized to be paid out of any moneys not otherwise appropriated, and to the sum of $15 per month during the residue of their natural lives. This provision shall apply to male and female alike. And all persons so released from servitude who shall be less than seventy years of age and of the age of sixty years or over, shall be entitled to receive the sum of $300, and also $12 per month until they shall reach the age of seventy years, when they shall be entitled to and receive the greater sum hereinbefore stated as a monthly payment. And all persons released from servitude as before stated who shall be less than sixty years old and of the age of fifty years or over shall be entitled to and receive the sum of $100 and also $8 per month, until sixty years old, when they shall receive $12. And all persons released from servitude as before stated who shall be less than fifty years of age, shall be entitled to and receive $4 per month until fifty years old, when they shall receive eight dollars. All moneys herein authorized to be paid shall be dispensed from the general funds of the treasury, not otherwise appropriated.

SEC. 3. Relations or others who may be charged with the support of aged or infirm persons released from involuntary servitude, in manner aforesaid, shall be entitled to and receive the monthly pension awarded to such aged or infirm persons in whole or in part upon showing to the satisfaction of the secretary of the interior that such support is afforded in a humane and becoming manner, the amount of such payment being under the control and direction of the secretary aforesaid.

SEC. 4. The secretary of the interior shall have power to prepare all needful rules and regulations for the carrying into effect of the provisions of this act according to the true intent and meaning thereof, and to designate proper officers or agents through whom freedmen and other persons may make application for payment and receive moneys authorized to be paid by the provisions of this act.

SEC. 5. All needful rules and regulations for the carrying into effect of the provisions of this act shall be approved by congress before the takeng into effect thereof.

SEC. 6. The compensation of agents charged with the enforcement of this law shall be recommended by the secretary of the interior and approved by congress.

SEC. 7. This act shall take effect and be in force from and after the first day of January, A. D. 1891.

The "Freedmen's Pension Bill," as it may be properly called, was introduced in the house of representatives June 24, 1890. It was read twice (which appears to be the custom) and referred to the Committee on Invalid Pensions. The following telegram was received as soon as the bill was introduced:

WASHINGTON, D. C., June 24, 1890.
Hon. W. R. Vaughan:

Your slave pension bill introduced and referred. Will send you copies as soon as printed.   W. J. CONNELL.

Congressman Connell's attention was immediately called to the fact that the bill should have been referred to the Committee on Pensions, and the following letter was promptly received:

HOUSE OF REPRESENTATIVES U. S., }
WASHINGTON, D. C., July 17, 1890. }
Hon. W. R. Vaughan:

DEAR SIR: I have before me your letter of the 8th instant acknowledging receipt of the copies of your Freedman's Bill, which I recently forwarded to you. You are correct in the statement that the bill has erroneously been referred to the Committee on Invalid Pensions. As you say, it should have been referred to the Committee on Pensions. I will at once have a change of reference made. As soon as this is done I will have a request made by the committee, in accordance with your suggestion, that the Secretary of the Interior furnish an estimate as to the probable cost to the government in carrying out the provisions of the bill. I will forward to you any references to the bill which I consider may be of special interest to you.

Very truly yours,

W. J. Connell

Possibly a reference to the Committee on Pensions, of which Representative DeLano is chairman, will secure a more ready consideration of the bill, as it is generally understood that the Pension Committee is not so burdened with business as the Invalid Pension Committee. Moreover, the claimants under the Freedman's Bill can scarcely be rated as invalids, except in those instances where they were soldiers and received disabilities by reason of wounds or disease. In such cases they would be pensioned as soldiers, but not because of their long service in bondage.

Of course there is a disposition to make light of this proposition in view of the "vast expense," according to the criticism of public prints. That expense will be less than 33 per cent. of the cost to the government of the great civil war, and from that heavy debt the country is emerging at the rate of $140,000,000 a year. Already the millionaires, and men of control in wealthy banking institutions, are howling at the prospect of the early payment of the national debt and there being left no means behind whereupon bonds may be predicated for the continuance of their pet institutions. It is respectfully suggested that justice to the negro might prove a panacea for the woes they have in such serious contemplation. What a pity it would be to let the poor millionaires fail of an opportunity to turn an honest penny.

THE CAUSE IS JUST.

Many of the metropolitan newspapers are owned by millionaires and they have attempted to burlesque the bill, claiming that the money requiring to pension the ex-slaves would bankrupt the government, etc. But hundreds of letters have been received by Mr. Connell and the author of the bill commending it as a measure of justice. As Congressman Connell expressed himself in the following letter on the subject of the cause being just, we take the liberty of reproducing his letter:

(See fac-simile of letter on following page.)

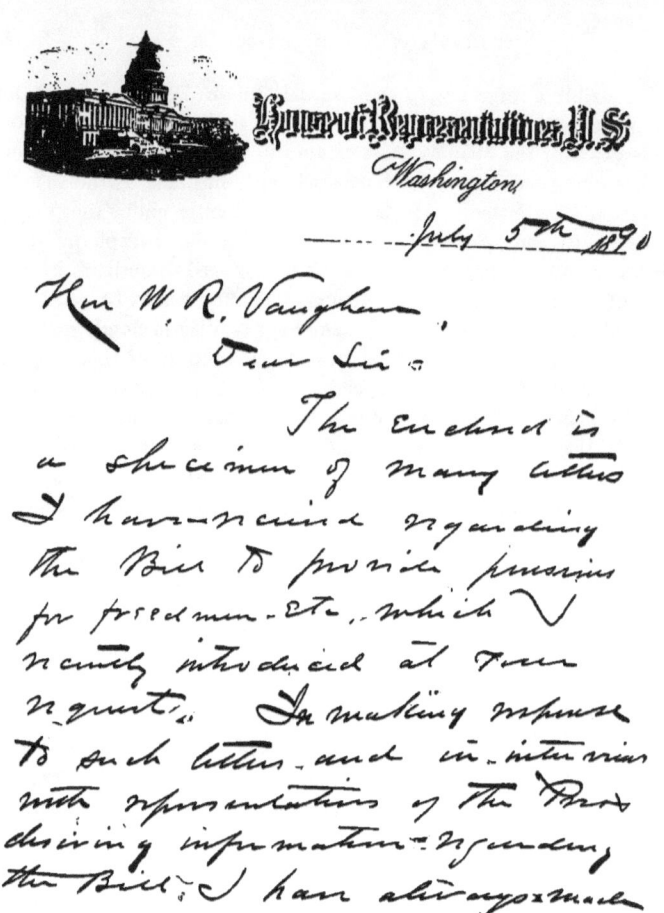

House of Representatives, U.S.

Washington,

————— July 5th 1890

Hon. W. R. Vaughan,

Dear Sir:

The enclosed is
a specimen of many letters
I have received regarding
the Bill to provide pensions
for freedmen-etc., which I
recently introduced at your
request. In making response
to such letters and in interviews
with representatives of the Press
desiring information regarding
the Bill; I have always made

[handwritten letter:]

mention of the fact that you
were the author of the Bill
and that I introduced it at
your request. As previously
stated, this I will make appear
in the Record in due time.
You are entitled to full
credit of both suggesting
and preparing the bill. Its
provision has, occasioned much
comment and some criticism.
But who cares for the latter
when the cause is just

Very Truly Yours,
W. J. Connell

The specimen letter to which Mr. Connell made reference in the foregoing communication was from Benjamin O. Jones, Esq., a gentleman of prominence in Southern Illinois, and was couched in the following terms:

METROPOLIS. ILL., June 27, 1890.

Hon. W. J. Connell, Washington, D. C.:

DEAR SIR: Allow me to congratulate you upon being the first man, in Congress, to take the initial step towards an act of justice to the ex-slaves of our country. Many thousands of slaves were thrown upon their own resources as a result of the war, and at a period of life when they were unable to learn the great problem of how to win bread. They have for years—those who survived— eked out a wretched existence at the hands of charity, unable to learn how to make a living. Many still survive in poverty, the inmates of our poor houses and other charitable institutions, or go among us as gaunt images of famine, a reproach to the government that made them freemen. Their condition was made wretched by the act of emancipation. They were taken away from abundance and turned out of their homes to starve. They helped to develop the resources and wealth of this country, and they ought to enjoy some of its blessings. They should not be allowed to fill paupers' graves or to seek at the hands of charity the commonest necessities of life. I am a white man, was raised in the slave state of Kentucky, and I desire to thank you for your noble courage and humanity in presenting this bill, in this prominent manner, to the consideration of the Congress of the United States.

Who would not prefer the dangers of a soldier's life to the torturing immolation of a life of slavery? Let us pension the old ex-slaves. I have advocated it on the stump, and I congratulate you that your position enables you to speak to more people and with greater effect. Please send me a copy of your bill.

Truly and sincerely,

BENJ. O. JONES.

Hundreds of letters from the white and colored citizens of the South have also been received, and the following is a fair sample of the southern sentiment as to "Vaughan's Freedmen's Pension Bill," for which reason it is reproduced:

SOUTHERN SENTIMENT.

SHERILL, ARK.. July 12, 1890.

W. R. Vaughan, Esq., Editor and President Omaha Democrat:

DEAR SIR: By accident, one of your valuable papers has fallen into my hands. Though, I guess, from the name, it is democratic in politics, yet it has the true ring of right and justice. I herein enclose subscription for daily and Sunday for one month, and intend to take it longer. I am a true blue republican, a colored man and an ex-slave. I am truly glad to see that there is *one* democrat that is a true friend from his heart to the negro that has been for years imposed upon. As for myself, I care not whether I get a cent from the government or not, as I was liberated when quite young, and am hale and hearty and able to take care of "me and mine." But justice should be done to the older ones, at least, who were turned loose at an old age, without education, homes or money, and broken down in health, unable to make a support, thrown upon the charity of a cold world—paupers. You and Congressman Connell, of your state, have enlisted in a humane and commendable cause. Whether you succeed or not, your names will be revered by the dusky sons of Africa as true friends of our race. The news of such a measure pensioning ex-slaves has spread among them like wildfire, and they are now watching with eager eyes, and listening with attentive ears, to see who their friends are, whether democrats or republicans.   Both parties tell us that they are our friends.   Well, we will wait, and see.   We will watch their votes.   Now is the time and opportunity to prove friendship.   The democratic party should vote for the measure, not because the negro is its ally, for he is not, but because it is right and just.   The republicans should support it for the same reasons, except the negro has been with *them* ever since Mr. Lincoln's proclamation.

The southern congressmen should support the bill for another reason beside justice, but because nine-tenths of the money will come south, and as most all of the merchants and land owners in the south are whites, of course it will circulate amongst them.   But we fear that for this reason my party (the republican) will defeat it.   We hope not.   In this matter of right and justice both parties should put themselves on record *unanimously* in favor of the bill.   Yours,   S. P. HAVIS.

The letters of Mr. Jones and S. P. Havis given above in full are inserted in these pages rather than any of the very many others which have been written upon the subject of the Freedmen's Pension Bill.   They commend Congressman Connell, who has taken the initiative in the work of justice towards an impoverished race, in his character as a representative of the people, and by Mr. Connell referred to the writer of these pages.   The fact is fully appreciated by the writer that courage, determination, and very possibly the expenditure of a good deal of money will be necessary in order to accomplish the great task now self-assumed. The aid of such a man as W. J. Connell, and of others who will give to him their confidence and support, will assist in the accomplishment of a work of reformation in governmental abuse which now warps the American character, as an avowed exponent of full and complete justice towards all men.   The words of commendation spoken and written to the author of the Freedmen's Pension Bill, would fill a fair sized volume; but the publication of all of these would be but a repetition, in substance of the candid words and views expressed in the communications of Mr. Jones and Mr. Havis.

If the writer could appeal to the better sentiment of the persons who make up the Commons of Great Britain, and to the men of liberal sentiment in that country, he would appeal to them to give their encouragement to an enterprise looking to a decent compensation to the sons and daughters of the race of human beings who were forced upon English colonists as slaves, years and years before American freedom from British domination was contemplated by even the most far-seeing and resolute of the American people. But such an appeal would probably be in vain. To the emancipated men and women of the recent slave states, however, it may be well enough to say: "Bear in remembrance the fact that you were not made slaves by the will of the people of the states that held you in bondage from your birth to the day of your liberation. You came to those people by inheritance. The institution of slavery was planted, nurtured and grew into power in American states under the authority and domination of the English nation when that power owned and ruled this land."

PROGRESS OF ANTI-SLAVERY SENTIMENT.

In another part of this volume it has been shown that the original importation of slaves into North America was the work of British merchants and traders, who forced the institution of slavery upon the colonies in violation of the protests of the colonists, who were averse to the establishment of the institution of slavery in their midst. Recurrence is had to this historical fact with a view of showing that there has always been a strong and able sentiment in opposition to the institution of human slavery; and that its apologists have been influenced by considerations of personal interest, coupled with an inability to make free the slaves, and to settle suitable provision for their sustenance upon the subjects of emancipation when made by masters to such as constituted their personal estate under the laws of those states where they severally resided.

From the best records obtainable it appears that British adventurers first engaged in the Importation of African slaves in the year 1562, during the reign of Queen Elizabeth, and that the scheme was undertaken for mercenary purposes. After Sir John Hawkins had made a profitable trip between the coast of Africa and the West India Islands, his monarch sent for him and upbraided him for engaging in an inhuman traffic; one that was "detestable" and would certainly "call down the vengeance of heaven." Although promising his queen not again to engage in a traffic in human flesh, he once more made a successful voyage to Africa, and returned with a cargo of Negroes who were impressed into slavery. Hill's Naval History tells us of Sir John Hawkins' second expedition, that "here began the horrid practice of forcing Africans into slavery, an injustice and barbarity which, so sure as there is a vengeance in heaven for the worst of crimes, will some time be the destruction of all who allow or encourage it.''

For two hundred years the slave trade was continued as a source of profit, and in the mean time it became firmly rooted upon the territory of the English colonies, and also upon the soil in possession of the governments of France and Spain. During all this period there were brave men who fought the iniquity with valor and determination. But like prudent men they did not seek to turn the world upside down at a single stroke. They directed their efforts, first towards the suppression of the slave trade, next to the prohibition of slavery extension upon free territory, and finally to the direction of the abolition of the institution itself.

Among the early enemies of the slave trade, and incidentally of human slavery, may be reconed Richard Baxter, the author of Baxter's Saints' Rest, and other works. of a christian and devotional character, who published a periodical known as the ''Negro and Indian Advocate.'' In the columns of his paper he took the ground that they who go out as pirates and take away African subjects or the people of any other land, who have never forfeited life or liberty, and make them slaves and sell them, are the worst of robbers, and ought to be considered as the common enemies of mankind. He went further and declared that they who buy them and use them as mere beasts for their own convenience, regardless of their spiritual welfare, are fitter to be called demons than christians.

At a later day Dr. Primatt published a lecture entitled a '' Dissertation on the Duty of Mercy,'' in which that eminent divine spoke of the institution of African slavery in the following scathing terms: '' It has pleased God to cover some men with white skins and others with black; but as there is neither merit nor demerit in complexion, the white man, notwithstanding the barbarity of custom and prejudice, can have no right by virtue of his color to enslave and tyrannize over the black man. For whether a man be white or black, such he is by God's appointment, and abstractly considered, is neither a subject for pride nor an object of contempt.''

In 1735 Dr. Atkins, a surgeon in the British navy, published an account of a voyage made by him to Guinea, on the west coast of Africa, and thence to the West Indies and Brazil. He describes vividly the methods pursued by slave dealers of supplying their vessels with their cargoes of human freight, by kid-napping. by false accusations and pretended trials, and every nefarious device known to avarice and cupidity. In his account he details the cruelties practiced upon the native Africans by white men, who were British slave traders; and he proceeds, while exposing their cruelty, to answer their staple argument, by which they maintained that the condition of the Africans was improved by their transportation to other countries.

Edmund Burke, the famous British statesman, in his account of the European settlements planted in America, placed upon record his observation that " the negroes in our colonies endure a slavery more complete, and attended with far worse circumstances, than what any people in their condition suffer in any other part of the world, or have suffered in any other period of time."

In the year 1766 Bishop Warburton preached a sermon before the Society for the Propagation of the Gospel, in which he dealt with slavery and the slave trade with an unsparing hand. He said : "From the free savages (the Indian tribes) I now come to the savages in bonds. By these I mean the vast multitudes yearly stolen from the opposite continent, and sacrificed by the colonists to their great idol, the god of gain. But what says these wor-shipers of Mammon? ' They are our own property which we offer up!' Gracious God! To talk, as of herds of cattle, of rational creatures, endowed with all our faculties, possessing all our qualities but that of color, our brethren both by nature and grace, shocks all the feelings of humanity, and the dictates of common sense. But alas! what is there in the abuse of society which does not shock them? Yet nothing is more certain in itself, and appa-rent to all, than that the infamous traffic in slaves directly infringes both divine and human law. Nature created man free, and grace invites him to assert his freedom. In excuse for this violation it has been pretended that though these miserable out-casts of humanity have been torn from their homes and native country by fraud and violence, yet they thereby become the happier, and their condition more eligible. But who are you, who pretend to judge of another man's happiness? Of that state which each man, under the guidance of his Maker, forms for himself, and not one man for another? To know what constitutes mine or your happiness is the sole prerogative of Him who created us, and cast us in so various and different moulds. Did your slaves ever complain to you of their unhappiness amidst their native woods and deserts? Or rather let me ask, did they ever cease complaining of their condition under you, their lordly masters, where they see indeed the accommodations of civil life but see them pass to others, themselves unbenefitted by them? Be so gracious, then, ye petty tyrants over human freedom, to let your slaves judge for themselves, what it is that makes their own happiness, and see if they do not place it in their return to their own country, rather than in the contemplation of your grandeur, of which their misery makes so large a part; a return so passionately longed for, that despairing of happiness here, that is, of escaping the chains of their cruel task-masters, they console themselves with feigning it to be the gracious reward of heaven in their future state."

Besides the captive Africans who were brought direct from their native shores to become serfs in the New World there were divers ways in which the institution of slavery was promulgated and fastened upon the pioneer settlers of nearly all the lands in the western hemisphere. To follow in detail these methods would be to write a volume equal in extent to the Holy Scriptures. But through all the vicissitudes of the poor negroes, who were constantly made the hewers of wood and the drawers of water for the white race, as the settlements of North and South America and adjacent islands increased, there were heard the voices of good men protesting against the wrong of slavery in the abstract and the horrors of the slave trade in particular. Among the noble men of England who interested themselves in their day for the betterment of the condition of the slaves, who became conspicuous by their determined opposition to the slave trade, may be mentioned Granville Sharp, who was instrumental, in 1772, in carrying the case of a slave, taken by his master from Jamaica to England, before the court of the Kings Bench, and there procured the decision of the judges "that as soon as ever any slave set his foot upon English territory he became free." Immediately after the trial Mr. Sharp wrote to Lord North, then principal minister of state, warning him, in the most earnest manner, to abolish immediately both the trade and the slavery of the human species in all the British dominions, as utterly irreconcilable with the principles of the British constitution and the established religion of the land.

Another powerful advocate of the national rights of man, appertaining to the black as well as the white race, appeared in the person of John Wesley, the celebrated divine. In 1774 this pious man took up the cause of the enslaved African race. He

had been to America and had seen and pitied the hard condition
of the slaves within the colonies of the mother country. He
published a work entitled " Thoughts on Slavery," which exerted
a salutary influence upon the public mind in riviting the convic-
tion that slavery was wrong, the slave trade abominable and that
both ought to be exterminated.

The Quakers of America early manifested a deep and com-
passionate feeling towards slaves within the American colonies,
although many of them became possessed of slave property upon
their settlement in this country. But it must be said of them that
they treated their slaves with great kindness. Notwithstanding
their mildness toward them, and the consequent content of the
slaves themselves, some of the society began to entertain doubts
in regard to the right of holding negroes in bondage at all.
Almost a century before the visit of John Wesley to America
some of the German Quakers, who had followed William Penn to
America, urged in the yearly meeting of Pennsylvania, the incon-
sistency of buying, selling and holding man in slavery, with the
principles of the Christian religion. At a later date the yearly
meeting for that province took up the subject as a public concern,
with the result that the society declared against the future impor-
tations of African slaves, and the members were charged to be
particularly attentive to the spiritual and temporal welfare of
those held in possession. For a series of years this solicitude was
renewed in the annual meetings, in fact being continued until the
institution of slavery had practically disappeared within the
province of Pennsylvania.

In the year 1772 a favorable disposition towards the condition of the slaves became manifest in several of the colonies. The
House of Burgesses of Virginia of that year presented a petition to
the King of Great Britain beseeching his majesty to remove all
those restraints on his governors of that colony which forbade
their assent to such laws as might check that inhuman and
impolitic commerce—the slave trade. It is a remarkable fact that
the refusal of the British government to permit the colonists to
exclude slaves from among them by law, was afterwards enumer-
ated by Thomas Jefferson among the public reasons for separating
from the mother country after the war of the revolution had
broken out.

In Mr. Jefferson's " Correspondence," there appears a fac-simile
of a portion of the original draft of the Declaration of Independence, which was stricken out of that document when it was

adopted in committee. The gentlemen selected in congress to prepare a formal document setting forth reasons why the colonies
should become free and independent states, were John Adams,
Thomas Jefferson, Benjamin Franklin, Roger Sherman and Robert
R. Livingston. To Mr. Jefferson was assigned the important duty
of preparing the form of the declaration. In his draft, submitted
to the whole committee, appears the following:

He (King George III. of England) has waged civil war against human
nature itself, violating the most sacred rights of life and liberty in the persons of a distant people, who never offended him; captivating and carrying them into slavery in another hemisphere, or to incur miserable death
in their transportation thither. This piratical warfare, the opprobrium
of infidel powers, is the warfare of the Christian King of Great Britain;
determined to keep open a market where MEN should be bought and sold,
he prostituted his negative for suppressing every legislative attempt to
prohibit or restrain this execrable commerce; and, that this assemblage
of horrors might want no fact of distinguished dye, he is now exciting
those very people to rise in arms among us, and to purchase that liberty
of which he has deprived them, by murdering the people upon whom he
has obtruded them, thus paying off former crimes, commi.ted against the
liberties of one people with crimes which he urges them to commit against
the lives of another.

It does not appear in Mr. Jefferson's works why the foregoing
indictment againt the English crown was stricken from the im-
mortal declaration, or which member of the committee moved its
expurgation. His wish not to reflect upon any of his co-patriots
in an hour of emergency no doubt prevented any personal reference to men on that solemn occasion. But all Americans know,
and the world knows, that Thomas Jefferson was a sincere devotee
of personal as well as collective liberty, and when he penned that
other great truth, which stands in the Declaration of Independence
as accepted, approved and signed in the colonial congress, that
" all men are born equal and endowed by their Creator with certain inalienable rights, among which are life, liberty and the pursuit of happiness," he meant the negro slave to be included side
by side with the white master, whose freedom was acknowledged
by all the world.

The facts set forth in this narrative amply demonstrate that
there was a strong sentiment both in Europe and America looking
to the curtailment of the slave power. which readily found expression in the Declaration of Independence, though not in the posi-
tive form that Mr. Jefferson desired. It is, however, enough to
know that when the cradle of American freedom was rocked our
patriot forefathers gave utterance to sentiments respecting universal liberty that included all races of men regardless of color.

From that day to the present there have been earnest men who have contended sincerely for the abridgment of slavery in every land.

Soon after the close of the revolutionary war the efforts of Wilberforce and the noble men who agreed with him in opinion secured the settled opposition of Great Britain to the continuance of the African slave trade. The adoption of the Constitution of the United States was the direct means of prohibiting the lawful introduction of impressed slaves into this country, and of putting an estoppel upon the trade altogether after 1808.

In the mean time President Jefferson concluded negotiations with Napoleon Bonaparte whereby the territory of Louisiana was purchased, which included nearly all the territory belonging to the United States, after the date of the purchase, lying west of the Mississippi river that gave early promise of seeking statehood within the Union. The cession of the Northwest Territory to the United States had been accompanied by an agreement in the congress of the confederation prior to the adoption of the constitution that such territory might be erected into seventeen states, when the population would admit of the formation of new states. Mr. Jefferson was chairman of the committee charged with framing an ordinance for the government of this vast area ; and during the session of 1784 he reported such an ordinance which contained the following rule:

That after the year 1800 of the Christian era, there shall be neither slavery nor involuntary servitude in any of said states, otherwise than in punishment of crimes whereof the party shall have been convicted to be personally guilty.

The rule was not then adopted, but in the last congress of the confederation Nathan Dane, of Massachusetts, reported an ordinance, July 11, 1787, for the government of the territory of the United States northwest of the Ohio river, in which the Jeffersonian interdiction of slavery was repeated, and it then received concurrence. All the great northwest was thereafter dedicated to freedom and became free soil.

It naturally follows that when the Louisiana purchase was made there was a strong feeling manifested to extend the Jeffersonian proviso to that territory. Unfortunately slavery existed therein before the purchase, and it could not be eradicated. But the agitation continued; and when the inhabitants of Missouri formed a state government, the same being a part of the Louisiana purchase, and applied for admission into the Union, during the month of March, 1818, the fact that the constitution of the new state recognized slavery caused the beginning of a fierce agitation which continued with more or less violence for nearly half a century. Missouri was not successful in her application at that time. In the next congress, November 16, 1820, Missouri again knocked for admission. The debate that ensued was long, fierce and acrimonious; but it was finally terminated February 27, 1821, by the admission of Missouri in pursuance of a compromise, which provided that in the erection of future new states those lying north of the parallel of 36° 30′ should be free states, and those lying south of that parallel might be free or slave as the people should elect.

The acceptance of the Missouri Compromise settled the status of slavery extension for thirty years. In 1850, when California applied for admission, the whole question of slavery extension was opened up, and with reference to the territory acquired from Mexico at the conclusion of the war with that government. Four years later the formation of territorial governments for Kansas and Nebraska revived the anti-slavery agitation with great bitterness. The repeal of the Missouri Compromise fired the northern heart to an extent that was not quieted again. The agitation was continued unceasingly and finally culminated in the election of Abraham Lincoln on a platform opposed to the acceptance of additional slave states in the Union. The civil war followed, and afterwards emancipation followed as a natural result.

The purpose of this imperfect review has been to show that there has always been an able and educated element in this country opposed to the bondage and oppression of the negro race, and that throughout the vicissitudes in the career of the black man as a slave, he has had powerful and eloquent champions, pleading with earnestness and fervor for his release from the galling chains of involuntary servitude. At last the day of freedom dawned in an unforseen and inexplicable manner. It came amidst the crash of systems that had been maintained in this land for three hundred years. It came in the din, the smoke and the carnage of battle. It came in a torrent of human blood, and through the havoc of mighty armies. It came as the will of Almighty God who selected this devastating agency to let the oppressed go free.

It is scarcely necessary to say that thousands of the men of the South would have willingly emancipated their slaves long years before the tocsin of war was sounded, but they were deterred therefrom in consequence of their pecuniary inability to set them up in life and make suitable provision for their maintenance in the first months or years of their struggle for existence. When emancipation was confirmed in the dread circumstance of war and subjugation, there was nothing to do but to accept the inevitable, and to recognize the fact that human slavery was a doomed institution for all the years of coming time. The men and women who were baptized in blood unto freedom went forth owing allegiance to none.

While blessing the day that has wiped out the curse of slavery from the escutcheon of our fair land, it is sad to contemplate that the wards of the nation are in a worse state to-day, so far as the personal comfort of thousands and tens of thousands of them are concerned, than they were in the days of their servitude. This is especially true of the old and infirm. In the hope that the government, which our fathers created and their sons here preserved, will dare to be just in defiance of obloquy, prejudice and ridicule, this humble appeal is made to those in place and power, for justice to the race that has been liberated from bondage, only that they may live in want and misery and die at last in nakedness and distress. Let the government be just. Generosity is not asked nor sought. Do what is right, and let the world know that the stars and stripes constitute the emblem of a nation that has the courage to correct the errors of ages. Let the spirit of the Vaughan ex-slave pension bill become the law of the land.

As a fitting finale to this petition for the rights of the slaves of olden days the following editorial from the columns of the Omaha Daily *Democrat*, of Sunday, August 13, 1890, is copied. W. R. Vaughan is president of the Democrat Publishing Company.

BE JUST AND FEAR NOT.

There are plainly those in political as well as in journalistic life who fear to discuss with fairness the provisions of Vaughan's Freedmen's Pension bill; and all such seek to underrate its importance by the idle declaration that it is a temporary expedient in government policy that will die under the breath of ridicule. A half century ago the same flimsy excuse for an argument was used by the public press and by political orators when James G. Birney entered the political arena as the candidate of the liberty party for the presidency. It was asserted that the meager support which Mr. Birney received in 1840—he had but little more than 7,000 votes in all the states—would deter the Garrison school of abolitionists from making another exhibition of their weakness, and that they would be glad to retire from public view never to expose themselves to familiar gaze again. But alas for human expectation when based upon nothing at all! The movement inaugurated by Birney, Garrison and their compatriots had substantial merit, and it gained accessions as the cause was discussed. In 1844 James G. Birney was again a presidential candidate and in that year he was given 62,000 votes, being considerably more than the plurality which James K. Polk received over Henry Clay. The liberty party began to be a noticeable feature in the affairs of the nation.

In 1848 Van Buren and Adams, under the name and guise of the free-soil party, received 291,000 votes in the several states. This was merely the old abolition party under a new name. The antipathy against the institution of slavery continued to spread, and finally culminated in the success of the republican party and in the emancipation of the slaves under the influences of a condition of war. Less than a quarter of a century after Birney and Garrison flung the banner of universal freedom to the breeze the institution of slavery had ceased to exist in the length and breadth of our fair land.

History, as Mr. Lincoln once said, is merely repeating itself. The demand for pensions in behalf of the former subjects of slavery is so fair and just that no opposition to the fundamental idea can weaken its merit; and attempts at ridicule will only give it a firmer hold upon the sense of justice entertained by a fair-minded people. In the face of weak pretension toward expression of contempt it will grow by day and by night until it has taken such deep root in the public mind that the law-making power of the United States will be glad to give it heed and obedience. In the poetic language of Charles Mackey it will become

"THE VOICE OF THE TIMES."

" Day unto day uttereth speech—
Be wise, oh ye nations, and hear
What yesterday telleth to-day—
    What to-day to-morrow will preach.
A change cometh over the sphere,
And the old goeth down to-day.
A new light hath dawned on the darkness of yore,
And men shall be slaves and oppressors no more.

" Hark to the throbbing of thought
In the breast of the wakening world;
Over land, over sea it hath come.
    The serf that was yesterday bought,
    To-day his defiance hath hurled—
No more is his slavery dumb—
He's broken away from the fetters that bind,
And he lifts a bold arm for the rights of mankind.

" The voice of opinion hath grown—
'Twas yesterday changeful and weak—
Like the voice of a boy in his prime.
    To-day it hath taken the tone
    Of an orator, worthy to speak—
Who knows the demand of his time!
To-morrow 'twill sound in the nation's dull ear
Like the trump of a seraph to startle our sphere.

" Be wise, oh ye rulers of earth!
And shut not your ears to his voice,
Nor allow it to warn you in vain.
    True Freedom, of yesterday's birth,
    Will march on its way and rejoice,
And never be conquered again.
This day hath a tongue—aye, the hours have speech—
Wise, wise will ye be if ye learn what they teach."

A question has arisen as to the history and character of the man who is willing to devote his time and means to the promulgation of a law that will do justice to the negro, without fee or reward to himself. That man is not ashamed of his name or of his public record, as far as he has one.

The following biographical sketch of

WALTER RALEIGH VAUGHAN

was published in the Omaha Daily Democrat of Sunday, June 20, 1890.

Since the appearance of the article given to the public last Sunday morning, proposing a pension to freedmen restored to liberty from a former condition of involuntary servitude, a large number of letters have been received from all quarters of the union, asking concerning the antecedents of ex-Mayor Vaughan and requesting a statement of the manner of man he is. In answer to these interrogatories a brief biographical sketch is given and a portrait of the man.

Walter Raleigh Vaughan was born in Petersburgh, Va., May 12, 1848. His parents moved to Montgomery, Ala., when the subject of this sketch was about one year old. His mother died in his second year, and at her request the babe was sent to reside with an uncle in North Carolina, the Rev. R. C. Maynard, who was a minister of the Methodist Episcopal persuasion. At the age of thirteen years young Vaughan returned to his father's home in Alabama.

From his early boyhood Mr. Vaughan became interested in labor and economic questions growing out of the condition of the laboring classes, upon whom his young eyes were naturally turned, white and black alike. Perhaps his first effort in the direct interest of the negro slave was made when, as a half-grown lad, he appealed to his father to give the negroes in bondage the half or the whole of Saturday of each week, to be used as his own time for private work or personal recreation. In all the later avocations of life Mr. Vaughan has contributed time and money whenever any important movement has been on the tapis in promoting the movements and wishes of the working classes. As an official and as a newspaper publisher, as well as in the private walks of life, he has advocated and aided the cause of labor and the aims of the men who have earned their own subsistence.

At the close of the war of the rebellion young Vaughan entered the Crittenden commercial college of Philadelphia, where he received a business education. He then took up his residence at St. Joseph, Mo., from whence he came to Omaha early in 1868 and booked himself as a guest of the old Herndon house at the foot of Farnam street, now the headquarters of the Union Pacific railway company. After a brief sojourn he located at Council Bluffs, Iowa, where he opened a business college. In that city, May 12, 1869, being the twenty-first anniversary of his birth, he was united in marriage with Miss Delia De Vol, daughter of one of the oldest residents.

In March, 1881, Mr. Vaughan was elected mayor of Council Bluffs, running as the regular democratic candidate, by a majority of thirty-six votes. In the meantime he had been actively engaged in business, a portion of it devoted to journalism, for which profession he has always had a penchant. In 1884 he was again elected mayor over a strong competitor by a majority of 588 votes. While serving as mayor, Gov. Larrabee, of Iowa duly appointed and commissioned him as one of the state curators, which position he resigned to remove to Omaha.

During Mayor Vaughan's first term in the mayoralty an unprecedented flood occurred in the Missouri river and all the lowlands were flooded and many families ruined by the devastation. Mayor Vaughan came to their rescue, had them gathered in boats from their flooded quarters and had them provided with food and other necessaries. As his term was about expiring, the well-remembered strikes were taking place in Omaha, wherein an old man named Armstrong was bayonetted by a soldier without cause or provocation. Mayor Vaughan at once sent a letter of condolence to the widow, together with a warranty deed to a residence lot in Council Bluffs, where the lady could make her home after her cruel bereavement.

During the second term of his mayoralty, in company with Mr. Thomas Officer, steps were taken to establish the Thompson-Houston electric light system in Council Bluffs, the twain being sole owners. Later on, with Mr. J. C. Regan for a partner, Mr. Vaughan secured a charter and established the electric light system of Omaha. His whole life has been checkered with business enterprises, having their ups and downs, but through all Mayor Vaughan has been steadfast in his adherence to the rights of the working classes.

After retiring from the mayoralty of Council Bluffs, Mr. Vaughan resumed his residence in Omaha, in which city he has had the general control and management of the *Omaha Daily Democrat.* In his capacity as a journalist he has now revived a project conceived by him years ago to have congress grant proper pensions to ex-slaves, whose early lives were made the subject of barter by citizens and taxation by the government. On this subject he carried on an extensive correspondence with public men seven years ago. Among them with President Harrison, who was then a senator from Indiana. None of the parties addressed appeared to view the project with favor. But, steadfast in his faith and in his belief in what he has conceived to be right, Mr. Vaughan proposes to go on in the line marked out until justice shall be done to a downtrodden people. It is only a question of time when his efforts shall succeed. An era different from being made the hewers of wood and the drawers of water for designing politicians is about to dawn upon the oppressed negro race. It will be an era of substantial prosperity.

As to the personality of W. R. Vaughan, it may be added that he was not a soldier during the late war, being then too young to bear arms. His father and three brothers were, however, gallant soldiers in the southern army. After the war of the rebellion had closed, his elder brother, Vernon H. Vaughan, was made secretary of Utah territory, at the request of Robert M. Douglas (son of the great Stephen A. Douglas), then private secretary of President Grant, and later United States marshal in North Carolina. The appointment was made by President Grant. When Gov. Shafer, of Utah, died, the president telegraphed the appointment of V. H. Vaughan to fill the vacancy without waiting to be officially informed that an appointment was required. Governor Vaughan died in later years in California. Mr. W. R. Vaughan is now in his 42d year, is the father of five sons and three daughters, all healthy, handsome children, and they are heart and soul with their father in his work for justice.

It is proper to say that since arriving at man's estate W. R. Vaughan has devoted much time and money in the upbuilding of benevolent and fraternal institutions. He was Noble Grand Arch of the United Ancient Order of Druids for the State of Iowa, and Grand Prelate of the Knights of Pythias organization for the same state, and he gave years of his best work to increase the powers and benefits of Odd Fellowship in the west, having been a patriarch since the age of 21 years.

Mr. Vaughan has a surviving brother, Alonzo Vaughan, now residing near Selma, Alabama. He has large landed interests in that vicinity and also conducts a mercantile business.

Let the writer make a closing appeal to the Christian people and the Benevolent orders of the United States by asking you to read

WHY THE FREEDMEN'S PENSION BILL SHOULD BECOME A LAW.

1. It will be a measure of recognition of the inhumanity practiced by the government in the holding, for a century, of men and women as slaves in defiance of human right.

2. It will be a slight recompense to emancipated freemen for the error of the government in permitting slavery to exist on the soil of a people whose fundamental idea is the liberty of the citizen.

3. It will afford to foreign nations a complete refutation of the sentiment, often advanced, that American Freedom has been merely a disguised form of tyranny whereof human slavery was an exemplification.

4. It will manifest to the civilized world the important truth that the Sons of the Fathers of the Republic associate liberty and justice together as inseparable in the administration of a government of the people.

5. It will afford a guaranty to other nations, struggling for popular independence, that the real strength of a free people lies in their ability to do right at all times and under all circumstances.

6. It will add to the material wealth of a great nation by giving to persons having a claim *de jure* against the government to put themselves in a position of complete equality before the law with other citizens whose personal rights have not been circumscribed.

7. It will enable an impoverished race, reduced to penury through no fault of their own, to place themselves in a position of

reasonable independence in their struggle for existence and recognition in general business affairs.

8. It will add to the national wealth of a productive section of the Union by enabling an important factor of its population to pursue business without constant appeals to public charity.

9. It will distribute a large addition to southern capital among a class of inhabitants who have been debarred hitherto from contributing to the general welfare of their section.

10. It will enable the emancipated race to contribute to the prosperity of their several states and to pursue avocations denied to persons wholly dependent upon their daily toil for support.

11. It will have a tendency to break down a residuary sense of race oppression which may have been fostered by means of a condition of dependence but a shade removed from the former condition of slavery.

12. It will remove the last barrier existing between the races which has made political solidity an objectionable feature in the political affairs of any section of the Great American Republic, and in coming years the thought of a solid North or a solid South will not have a shade of sectional support.

13. It will be the duty of public men, it is hoped, occupying every station of life, whether in the Senate or the House, whether the president or governors of states, whether judges of courts or attorneys at the bar, whether bankers or managers of great corporations of every class, to ask themselves whether this claim of one-tenth of the population of the United States ought to be disregarded, and whether any country can continually prosper that suffers injustice to such a large part of its people.

As you should be judged by the future generations of your countrymen, and finally by the All Wise Arbiter of human accounts, you are adjured not to turn a deaf ear to the petition now made in behalf of a misused and selfishly derided race, which has been emancipated from bondage only to be wedded to lives of ignorance and a condition of penury bordering upon starvation. In the name and hope of that justice which ought to animate the hearts of all true men, let the appeal sink deep into your minds, to the end that you shall heed the call made upon you to encourage an earnest support of the Freedmen's Pension Bill. "As ye would that men should do to you, do ye even so to them."

WALTER R. VAUGHAN.

FREED, UNEDUCATED, NO MONEY AND NO FRIENDS—RAGS AND POVERTY
HIS PORTION.

MEN OF MERIT.

In the foregoing pages it has been intended to show, in as brief a compass as may be considered consistent with a proper delineation of the general character of negroes as citizens, something of their fealty to their masters in the days of slavery, their devotion to the cause of liberty when they found the way opened for them to become freemen, their success in life when thrown upon their own resources, their heroic bravery in the Union cause when mustered into the Federal service in the capacity of soldiers, and their honorable reputation as statesmen in cases where colored men have been called into the political field. To this it might have been added that very many of them have risen to distinction in the Christian church and in the field of letters. But this branch of the subject may be fittingly discussed in a series of brief biographical sketches of men who have achieved distinction in their capacity as freemen after having been liberated from the bonds of slavery.

Before entering upon the narration of individual cases it may be proper to say that almost every community of the South has within it some person who ought to rank as a hero, but who is unknown to fame because there has been a desire to enjoy the blessings of domestic life rather than to engage in a calling that would bring an individual into public notice. Very many of the emancipated slaves have discovered decided financial ability, and they have accumulated large wealth. Mr. Montgomery, who was trusted slave of Jefferson Davis, under the old regime, and who acted as his quarter's agent in very many important commercial transactions, accumulated an extensive property after he became a freeman, and was widely known as an enterprising and successful planter. He is but one of many whose talent ran in the line of trade and traffic. The instances of slaves made freemen, with no resources but the talents which God gave to them, but who have acquired a competency, would fill a large volume.

Recently the writer was much interested in perusing a newspaper sketch of a negro lad in Mississippi, who attracted the attention of his mistress by marks of natural shrewdness, and the lady conceived the idea of his being made useful to her in other lines than in a life of drudgery, provided he possessed a fair degree of

cultivation. She thereupon devoted a short time every morning
in teaching the boy to read. He was apt in learning, and in a
comparatively short time he had acquired the rudiments of a fair
English education, with no other instruction than such as his mistress was able to impart. While conditions were as stated the
civil war broke out. The adult white members of the family in
which the young negro was held as a slave, three in number, all
entered the Confederate army, and in the vicissitudes of the war
they all fell. Towards the close of hostilities the old plantation
suffered from the incursions of contending armies, and became the
prey of foraging parties on both sides. Tribute was levied first by
the one and then by the other. In a season of ruthless devastation
the improvements upon the plantation were destroyed by fire.
Peace came, but the old mistress was impoverished — nothing re-
maining to her except her barren acres. These were mortgaged
in a hopeless struggle to improve the place and begin life anew;
but the effort was fruitless, and the mortgage, in due time, ate up
the land. The plantation passed under the hammer. In some
manner the slave boy of former years learned that his old home
was to be sold, and that his kind mistress was about to meet the
cold charity of the world as a beggar. Like thousands of others
of his race he had enlisted in the Union service, and after discharge
he had been engaged in a struggle for fortune, and had been moder-
ately successful. He turned his face toward the old plantation and
arrived at the county seat in time to attend the sale. As if
divinely ordered he became the successful bidder, and the place
whereon his eyes first beheld the light of day became his property
in fee simple. His next step was to hunt up his old mistress and
to minister to her comfort. She had relatives living in Virginia
and the desire of her heart seemed to be that she might be able to
reach them and to die amidst the scenes of her childhood. Her former servant provided the means, and the lady returned to her native state. The bright boy she had taught to read became a planter
on the estate where he had once toiled as a slave. He rebuilt the
houses, raised his crops and prospered in the new life. Every year
he sent a handsome donation to his former mistress, which he increased in amount as his circumstances improved. The young man
became very wealthy, buying other plantations, and giving employment to many of his former fellow-slaves. He still lives and
is rated to be worth a half million of money. His old mistress is
also living, made comfortable in her old age by the munificence of
the man who once ranked as one of her chattels. Every month this

kind-hearted freedman sends his old mistress a check for one hundred and fifty dollars, and he will continue to do so until she is called to the better land.

This incident has been related at length for the reason that it affords a good illustration of that genuine love which is an inherent part of the negro character. Unquestionably there are to be found throughout the South thousands of such instances of unselfish devotion on the part of the ex-slaves for the surviving members of the families of their old-time masters. The truth of such an assumption is rendered highly probable by one circumstance that admits of no dispute. The great mass of the ex-slaves have remained within near approach to the scenes of their former servitude. They do so from a dislike to break up and destroy the associations of early years. Of course there has been a great shifting of scenes on the part of many; and in some instances mammoth emigration associations have been organized of those who have sought new homes in distant states and territories. But the number who sought new locations probably amounts to no more than ten per cent. of the emancipated people.

The humble walks of life furnish as many evidences of great hearts among the southern freedmen as may be shown by those who have risen to eminence in church and state. But being unknown it is not an easy matter to do them that degree of justice which their gratitude and devotion are entitled to receive. In this respect the Negro stands side by side with the white man. Of the Anglo-Saxon races, and, indeed, of all races of men, it is the eminent few who are named in history, while the humble many run their course and go to the grave unknown, unhonored and unsung.

But for the purpose of manifesting the progress which the Negro has made under very trying circumstances, a brief review of the lives of some of the noted men of the race, will be in order.

From the beginning it has been the purpose of this little volume to confine its narration to those persons of color, in the main, who have been the subjects of slavery within the United States, with a view of exhibiting their heroism in rising above the rule of oppression, that was their birthright, and of the years of their early lives. There have been many free men of color who were never held as slaves who have been an honor to their race, but these scarcely come within the line of this discussion.

CRISPUS ATTUCKS.

In a former part of this volume it has been shown that at the time of the foundation of the federal constitution all of the states held slaves except one. Prior to that date, in colonial days and before the old French war, slaves were held in all communities settled by immigration from Europe. About the year 1723 there was born of a slave mother in the colony of Massachusetts the subject of this sketch, Crispus Attucks. Like all men possessing natural aspirations for liberty, Crispus Attucks chafed under the rule of slavery and longed to be free. When he was 27 years old he managed to escape from his master at Farmington, the date of his escape being September 30, 1750. He has been described as a finely developed man, of a bright yellow complexion, six feet two inches in height, broad shouldered and in every respect an athlete. He had learned to read, for at that time the education of a slave was not entirely forbidden. His master advertised for his recovery, offering a reward of ten pounds sterling for his capture. As it was presumed he would try 'to go abroad in some sailing vessel all masters of such vessels and others were cautioned "against concealing or carrying off said servant on penalty of the law." But the caution was useless, for Crispus Attucks made good his escape and was not captured.

His biographers do not tell us whether he went to sea or fled to the forests, or how he managed to survive, but it is certain that the soul-born love of freedom which he cherished was not quenched. He was ready to fight for liberty, and if need be, to die for the cause, not for himself alone, but for all the subjects of oppression. And in that manner he met his death.

The Boston massacre took place March 5, 1770. The inhabitants of that city had been the victims of British oppression to a degree that frenzied them with madness. They had been taxed without representation, and at last British troops were sent among them to enforce subjection at the point of the bayonet. They formed clubs to drive out the invaders. Shouting, "let us drive out the ribalds — they have no business here," the crowd rushed toward King street and made for the custom-house. At the sight of an armed sentinel the mob shouted, "Kill him! kill him!" and made an attack. Charles Botta, the Italian historian says: "There was a band of the populace, led by a mulatto named Attucks, who brandished their clubs and pelted them with snow-balls. The soldiers received the advance of the populace at the point of their bayonets. The scene was horrible. At length the mulatto and twelve of his companions pressing forward environed the soldiers, striking their muskets with their clubs, cried to the multitude, 'Be not afraid—they dare not fire. Why do you hesitate? Why do you not kill them? Why not crush them out at once?' ''

Inspired by the words of Attucks the crowd rushed madly on and, as they approached the soldiery, there was a discharge of firearms. Attucks, the brave leader, had lifted his arm to strike down Capt. Preston, the British officer in command, but he fell a victim to the first·gun shot. Two others fell with him and five were wounded. The cry of bloodshed spread like wild fire. Citizens crowded the streets, white with rage. The church-bells rang the alarm, and in a little while the whole country was aroused to battle.

Crispus Attucks was buried from historic Fanueil Hall with pomp and honor. He was no longer looked upon as a fugitive slave on whose head a price had been set, but as a patriot leader who had dared to shed his blood in defiance of British oppression. His position had been taken with firmness and decision, for in advance of the massacre he had addressed a letter to the Tory Governor of the provice of Massachusetts in these words:

SIR: You will hear from us with astonishment. You ought to hear from us with horror. You are chargeable before God and man with our blood. The soldiers are but passive instruments, mere machines, neither moral or voluntary agents in our destruction, more than the leaden pellets with which we were wounded. You were a free agent. You acted coolly, deliberately, with all that premeditated malice, not against us in particular, but against the people in general, which, in sight of the law, is an ingredient in the composition of murder. You will hear from us further hereafter.   CRISPUS ATTUCKS.

This letter has reference to a former skirmish before the fatal day of massacre.

It will thus be seen that the first blood shed in the cause of the American Revolution was that of a patriot man of color who had lived twenty years of freedom after having deliberately broken the chains that bound him to a life of slavery. Where Crispus Attucks had made his abode during those twenty years has not been made known to the present generation. Although a price had been set upon his head it is manifest that he did not go far enough away from Boston to prevent his hearing the clanking of the chains that were being forged to make Americans of every creed and color the slaves of British tyranny. At the first manifestation of force he placed himself at the head of the people by right of having been born and ordained of God as a natural

leader of men. He fell a martyr in a holy cause.   Let his name
be held in sacred endearment.

The history of Crispus Attucks gives evidence that slaves are
entitled to freedom, and they deserve compensation for the labor
they performed when their time was not their own.

FREDERICK DOUGLASS.

Perhaps the best known man of color, now living, and the man
of all others who has been regarded as the representative man of
his race, is Frederick Douglass.   A biographical sketch of this
remarkable negro reads more like romance than fact; and yet
every word that has been published respecting him is fact without
the half having been told.

'Mr. Douglass does not know his exact age, but he was probably
born in the year 1817 or 1818.   In an interview with his old
master, who once held him as a slave, a few months prior to the
death of the latter, he was told that according to the recollection
of Captain Auld, he was born in the month of February, 1818.
He had always regarded himself one year older.   The birthplace
of Douglass was in the district of Tuckahoe on the eastern shore
of Maryland.   His early years were marked by extreme poverty
and wretchedness.   He was the slave of Captain Auld, who was a
severe taskmaster and selfishly cruel.   Southern slave holders were
not generally cruel, but there were exceptions, and the case of
Frederick Douglass constituted an extraordinary exception.

When ten years old Douglass was sent to Mrs. Sophia Auld,
a relation by marriage to Captain Auld, to be reared as a
house servant in Baltimore.   His situation was now greatly
improved.   The woman had humane characteristics, and noticing
that her servant was naturally bright and quick she began teaching him the alphabet.   But her husband ascertained what was
going on and soon put a stop to further instruction.   Possibly
this circumstance changed the whole tenor of Frederick Douglass'
life.   Had Mrs. Auld been permitted to teach him to read, and to
have given him that kindly treatment which her heart prompted,
he might have been content to have remained in Baltimore, and
he would have endured a life of slavery as millions of others have
done.   But the inhibition of the instruction he craved, only
whetted his appetite for learning, and excited a determination to
be a free man at the earliest opportunity.   He carried his spelling
book in his jacket and by sheer effort taught himself.   When he
could read a little he invested his little earnings in a copy of the

FREDERICK DOUGLASS.

old Columbian Orator, and after reading the "Fanaticism of Liberty" and the "Declaration of Independence" he made up his mind that there was no just right in holding him in slavery. He watched his chance and ran away. He had by this time nearly reached his majority and was engaged to a free woman of color. He made his way, as best he could, to New York, whither his affianced wife followed him. They were married and settled at New Bedford, Mass. Here he pursued a life of the severest toil, doing any job of work he could procure. Here several of his children were born. Through all his toil he continued his studies and developed an active mind that will compare favorably with the educated talent of our first statesmen. He was a regular reader of William Lloyd Garrison's Liberator, and gauged his career after the system of that gentleman's teachings.

His first political address was delivered at Nantucket in 1841. He was at once made an agent of the American Anti-Slavery society, and in that capacity he began a crusade for the freedom and elevation of his race. His reputation began to extend all over the states and to foreign countries. The rumor went abroad that he was a fugitive from slavery, and there were constant threats of his arrest. But his identity was not easily established, as he had assumed the name of Frederick Douglass, and was not suspected of being the runaway slave of Capt. Auld. The custom of slave days was for the servant to bear the name of the master.

As his oratorical career spread his fame abroad Mr. Douglass was pressed to visit England in the advancement of his work. There he was lionized. He was the guest of John Bright and British statesmen delighted to do him honor. He subsequently engaged in journalism and was the editor of several publications. While publishing Frederick Douglass' Paper he conceived the idea of sending his journal to every member of congress, which he did for several years.

About this time Mr. Douglass made the acquaintance of John Brown, of Harper's Ferry memory, and they became fast friends. Together they formed plans for the liberation of slaves, but Mr. Douglass did not approve of an armed insurrection and did his best to induce Mr. Brown to abandon that program. In this, as the world knows, he was not successful. Had Mr. Douglass been successful in changing Mr. Brown's plans the Harper's Ferry tragedy would not have occurred.

The association between Frederick Douglass and Mr. Brown became known, and with it the information was imparted as to

Mr. Douglass' identity. Governor Wise, of Virginia, took measures to have him arrested and restored to slavery. He addressed a letter to President Buchanan, asking to have two detectives commissioned as special mail agents that they might shadow him and, when convenient, arrest and take him south. But the facts came to light, and acting under the advice of friends Mr. Douglass repaired to Canada and thence sailed for Europe. He remained abroad until he might safely return to America and resume his anti-slavery work at home.

During the war Mr. Douglass was a prominent figure in all that appertained to his race. He urged the issue of the emancipation proclamation with all the vigor and force of his great intellect, and when Mr. Lincoln finally became persuaded that emancipation, as a war measure, was a union necessity he proceeded to act. When the first proclamation of September 1862 was made public, it is probable that no happier man lived on American soil than Frederick Douglass. The work of a lifetime was accomplished, the prayers of a lifetime had been answered, and the oppressed people of his race were practically free.

Naturally, a man of Mr. Douglass' patriotic views on national questions, and his great desire to see his race elevated to a high standard of respectability, caused him to take a deep interest in the purposes of the war during its continuance. He was among the first to encourage the enlistment of colored troops, and to have them put upon a footing with white soldiers. He had become a man of large wealth, and he used his private means freely in the organization of black regiments, and in equipping the troops for service in the field. Two of his sons were among the first to enlist and thousands of others went with them to the front. While the young men of his race were taking part in active service, Mr. Douglass interested himself in securing for the negro troops the right of exchange and the general humane treatment extended to captives taken in war. In this work he was successful in a marked degree.

After the conclusion of hostilities Mr. Douglass was an active participant in the exciting scenes that took place in congress and other legislative bodies looking to riveting the rights established for the negro race upon the federal constitution, and the constitutions of those states wherein slavery had previously been a recognized institution. He was very active and influential in procuring the passage of the fourteenth and fifteenth amendments to the federal constitution, the freedmen's bureau bill, the civil rights act and other legislation necessary for the peace, comfort and protection of his race.

Following the busy scenes and events of the reconstruction period Mr. Douglass entered the lecture field and achieved great distinction as a platform orator. In this theater of action he encountered much of the prejudice entertained by white people against the black race, simply because of their color. Great crowds rushed to hear him discuss the civic questions of the day, but very few desired to care for his comfort and well-being as he filled his lecture engagements. All were anxious to hear, but scarcely any were willing to entertain. An incident of this character is worth relating.

Mr. Douglass had been invited to lecture before the library association at Evansville, Indiana. The question arose, "What shall we do with him?" None of the gentlemen directly connected with the association cared to have him as a guest. By chance Col. A. T. Whittlesey, who had been postmaster at Evansville during the administration of President Johnson, and was then the editor of the Evansville Daily Courier, and now of the Omaha Daily Democrat, learned of a heated discussion upon the subject between gentlemen of political sympathy with Mr. Douglass, not one of whom were willing to open their doors to the great orator. Col. Whittlesey at once addressed a note to Dr. H. W. Cloud, of the lecture committee, stating that he would be glad to have Mr. Douglass become his guest, and that all colored persons, ladies and gentlemen, who desired to pay their respects to Mr. Douglass during his sojourn would be just as welcome at his parlors as white persons who might see fit to call.

Mr. Whittlesey and his wife had frequently entertained such eminent statesmen as Thomas A. Hendricks, Senator Voorhees and other persons of recognized political reputation. It was remarked that as their guest Mr. Douglass would be extended all the courtesy and attention due to his great ability, but for political reasons party leaders refused to permit the proposed arrangement to be carried out. Mr. Douglass was not allowed to be Col. Whittlesey's guest, nor the guest of any other respectable white gentleman in Evansville. Neither was he provided with quarters in any of the public hotels in the city. He was accommodated at a negro boarding house kept by a Widow Carter, a very highly respected colored lady, and no white persons called to pay their respects other than the lecture committee having him immediately under their charge. It is scarcely necessary to say that this little episode created an intense local excitement for a time, and it serves to show the deep seated prejudice entertained against the colored race, even at the North, by persons claiming to be the especial friends and champions of the blacks.   But this prejudice is fast disappearing, and a feeling of brotherly kindness and regard is gradually extending.

In the civil service since the war Mr. Douglass has been a ry conspicuous figure.   He was a presidential elector in the state of New York in 1872, was made Marshal of the District of Columbia in 1877 and Register of Deeds of the District in 1881. He continued to hold that office about a year and a half under the administration of President Cleveland.   He is now American Minister at San Domingo.   He is in all respects a great man, having few equals in any walk of life.   He is purely a self-made man, and he has raised himself to the top-most round of the ladder of fame.   He is a credit to the negro race and an honor to any people.

SAMUEL R. LOWERY.

The subject of this sketch is a person of a different cast in life from most of the others who have made a record for distinguishment in the annals of the black race.   While descended from slave stock, on the one side, he was not himself a slave, his mother having been a free woman from the time of his birth.   But his father was a slave, and never breathed the air of personal freedom until the edict of emancipation was promulgated.   He was then at liberty to meet his distinguished son on the plane of liberty, which is the natural right of all men without regard to color.

Samuel R. Lowery was born December 9, 1830, from the union of a slave father and a mother who was a full-blooded Cherokee Indian.   The father is living, or was two years ago, at Nashville, Tenn., and in all that goodly city there is no man who has a juster pride in his offspring than Father Lowery entertains for the progress made by his distinguished son.   Mr. Lowery lost his mother when he was about eight years old.   At the age of sixteen years Mr. Lowery took upon himself the business of school teaching, and for one so young met with tolerable success, and continued to teach until he was twenty years old.   During his course as a teacher he fell in with Rev. Talbot Fanning, who aided the young man in his aspirations and was instrumental in securing for him a good education.   He entered the, ministry and for about eight years was pastor of the

SAMUEL R. LOWERY.

Christian church at Cincinnati, Ohio. While following the life of a Christian minister in the Queen City he married a colored lady of culture, and soon afterward took up his residence in Canada. He returned to the United States in 1863, after the appearance of President Lincoln's second proclamation, and proceeding to Nashville, near the scenes of his birthplace, he began preaching the doctrine of salvation as taught in the Christian churches, but he coupled with it the freedom of the southern slaves as an incident of salvation. He became chaplain of Col. Crawford's regiment of negro soldiers, the same being the Fortieth regiment of the United States infantry regulars. He was afterward transferred to the Ninth United States heavy artillery, with which he remained in the capacity of chaplain until the dawn of peace.

Mr. Lowery opened a school in Rutherford county, Tennessee, after the war, but the prevalence of political excitement prevented his success in that work. He then took a law course and was admitted to the bar at Nashville. In 1875 he took up his residence at Huntsville, Alabama, and pursued his legal calling with marked success. One of his cases having been carried to the supreme court of the United States he followed it to Washington for the purpose of making an argument, and he was admitted to the bar of the highest tribunal of the land upon motion of Mrs. Belva A. Lockwood, the renowned female attorney. While in Washington his two daughters, aged respectively 15 and 10 years, visited an exhibition of silkworms and became interested in the silk culture. They persuaded their father to purchase some silkworm eggs, which he did, and with the aid of the southern mulberry tree as a feeder of the worms Mr. Lowery began the silk culture at Huntsville, which he has promoted to a valuable industry. After beginning this work Mr. Lowery visited all the silk industries in America and mastered all the points to which his attention was directed.

Mr. Lowery has abandoned the practice of the law and has given his whole time to the culture of silk. At the New Orleans industrial exposition he was awarded the first prize for fine silk goods, over an old French establishment to which a premium of $1,000 had been paid as an inducement to make an exhibit. The silk factory at Huntsville is in a very prosperous condition, and the name of Samuel R. Lowery, preacher, lawyer and manufacturer, is among those standing high in the progress of the colored people. His father was a slave!

HON. ROBERT SMALLS.

Few of the ex-slaves deserve more favorable mention or higher honor than the ex-member of Congress from the Beaufort district of South Carolina. Mr. Smalls was born at Beaufort, in the district which he subsequently represented in the house of representatives at Washington, April 5, 1839. As a slave his advantages of education were limited, but by hook or crook he managed to secure the smattering of an English education. In 1851 he went to Charleston and was employed in the business of ship rigging. In this business he learned the business of equipping a vessel and incidentally the duties of a sailor. In that capacity he became connected with the Planter, a transport doing business in Charleston harbor. He was employed on board that vessel when Fort Sumter was fired upon in 1861. The Planter was taken in possession by the Confederate authorities and was used as a dispatch boat until she was captured and turned over to the blockading fleet of the United States navy, May 13, 1862.

The capture of the vessel was accomplished by Robert Smalls. The day before, the vessel had been engaged in removing guns from Coles Island to James Island. After the work was done the boat returned to Charleston. The officers went ashore, leaving a crew of eight colored men on board in charge of Mr. Smalls, who was a wheelman and acting pilot. The crew was called together, and Robert Smalls laid before the men on deck his plan for turning over the vessel to the United States squadron, to which all assented, although two of the men became frightened and concluded to remain behind. The scheme was hazardous, as the boat was obliged to pass under the guns of the fort and the shore batteries. Detection was certain death. At 2 o'clock in the morning steam was raised and the Planter, with a valuable cargo of guns and ammunition, designed for the equipment of Fort Ripley, a new fortification erected in the harbor, moved up to the North Atlantic wharf, where Smalls' wife and two children, three men and four other women, were taken on board. All were colored people. The Planter passed Fort Johnson, first sounding her whistle in salute, and receiving the customary salute in return, and proceeded down the bay. Passing Fort Sumter Smalls leaned out of the pilot house with the broad sombrero of Relay, the master of the vessel, drawn over his face, and was mistaken for that officer.

The required signal was given and responded to. After passing the Fort the Planter was headed for Morris Island, then

HON. ROBERT SMALLS.

occupied by Hatch's light artillery. When it became evident that
the Planter was heading for the Federal fleet the Hatch battery at
Morris' Island was signalled to stop her; but it was too late. The
Planter displayed a white flag, but in the darkness it was not distinguished. She was mistaken for a Confederate ram, and the
naval vessels drew out of her way. The ship Onward, not being a
steamer, prepared for a broadside, when the lookout chanced to
observe the flag of truce. When within hailing distance her character was explained and the Planter was speedily surrendered to
Captain Nichols, of the United States navy. Robert Smalls was
afterwards transferred to the gun-boat Crusader, and on board of
that vessel and the captured Planter he continued to do duty during the war. He was honored with a captain's rank in the United
States navy, but he was never commissioned as such an officer.

After the war a bill was introduced in Congress to place the
name of Robert Smalls upon the retired list of the United States
navy, and a voluminous report was submitted showing the value of
the property which he captured, and the meritorious service which
he rendered to the Government of the United States. Yet, strange
to say, the bill did not pass for the frivolous reason assigned that
there was no precedent for placing a civilian upon the retired list of
the navy.   Had Mr. Smalls been a distinguished politician of the
party in power he would, no doubt, have been voted a high reward
for services rendered the Union cause.

At the close of the war Captain Smalls, as he was called, drop-
ped, naturally, into civil life. He was elected a member of the
convention which framed the constitution of South Carolina under
the reconstruction acts, and took an active part in the proceedings.
In 1868 he was made a member of the state legislature, and was the
author of the state civil rights bill. He then served a part of a
term in the state senate as the successor of Judge Wright, and afterwards was elected for a full term. He occupied a high rank in the
South Carolina militia, holding the rank of lieutenant-colonel of
the third regiment, and was made a brigadier-general in 1873.

General Smalls was a delegate to three national conventions of
the republican party—at Philadelphia, in 1872, when Grant and
Wilson received the party nomination; at Cincinnati, in 1876,
when Hayes and Wheeler were nominated, and again at Chicago,
in 1884, when Blaine and Logan were placed in the field. He has
served three successive terms in Congress, having been elected the
first time in 1880, to the Forty-seventh Congress; he was re-elected
in 1882 to the Forty-eighth Congress, and again in 1884 to the

Forty-ninth Congress. He is a gentleman of pleasant demeanor, affable and approachable, and he is in every respect an honor to his race.

PROF. JOSEPH E. JONES.

Among the remarkable men, of the African race who have sprung from the lap of the institution of slavery, there are some who have distinguished themselves in the field of literature and learning in a high degree, and have made a mark in educational progress quite as eminent as those who have taken a high rank in political life. In this catalogue very honorable mention deserves to be made of Prof. J. E. Jones, of the theological seminary at Richmond, Virginia.

Prof. Jones was born in slavery in the city of Lynchburg, October 15, 1850. He is still a comparatively young man. He began life at the age of six years, as stripper in a tobacco factory, greatly to the disgust of his mother, who had a mother's heart and ambition for her offspring. The laws of Virginia forbade the education of slaves, and there opened up for the mother only a life of toil for her boy. Yet she conceived the idea that some time in the future the negroes would become free, and that her son would be somebody. She frequently expressed such sentiments to her fellow slaves, and on one occasion she stated her opinion to her master. The woman was esteemed to be stark mad. There was, however, method in her madness, and having saved some money of her own, she procured the services of a negro in the same family to which she belonged, but who had a limited education, to give her son elementary lessons. Two or three evenings a week were devoted to this purpose. It was near the end of the war, in 1864, and the condition of the confederate cause was becoming desperate. The teacher became frightened and concluded that it would be prudent for him to suspend his educational functions. After much persuasion he concluded to continue the lessons every Sunday morning from 10 to 12 o'clock. About this time the teacher's owner ascertained that his slave could read and write, and the master accordingly sold a slave that was such unsafe property as to be possessed of a little education. This was a sad blow to the aspirations of young Joe Jones.

But the fond mother could not give over her project of securing an education for her son. A sick confederate soldier happened to come in her locality and she offered him lodging and food in case he would give lessons to the young lad. Thus matters continued for several weeks until the surrender of General Lee at

PROF. JOSEPH E. JONES.

Appomattox. Then followed the universal recognition of the success of emancipation, and a brighter day dawned for the aspiring youth. He at once became a student in a private school opened at Lynchburg, where he continued two years.

In October, 1868, young Jones entered the Richmond Institute, now the Richmond Seminary, in which he figures as a Professor. Here he received instruction three years and then entered the Madison University at Hamilton, N. Y., where he graduated in 1876, having taken a complete preparatory and college course. The same year the American Baptist Home Mission Society, of New York, appointed him as instructor in the Richmond Institute, and made him professor of language and philosophy. The following year he was ordained as a Baptist Minister, and his Alma Mater conferred upon him the degree of Master of Arts. He is now professor of Homeletics and the Greek language in the Richmond Theological Seminary.

The career of this able and accomplished student furnishes abundant evidence that the despised negro slave of other days may become eminent in letters and renowned in the service of the Divine Master.

PROF. JOHN H. BURRUS.

The surrender of 1865 found three slave boys named Burrus at Marshall, Texas, with the remnant of Bragg's army. With their mother they were sent to Shreveport, La., thence to New Orleans and finally to Memphis, Tenn. Here the subject of this sketch, John H. Burrus found employment as a steamboat cook. About 1866 he went to Nashville and became a hotel waiter. He saved his money and took to study of evenings in order to acquire an education, receiving instruction from two lady boarders of the hotel. By 1867 he had saved $300, and then determined to take a course at the Fisk University. During the vacations he taught school. Thus he continued until 1874. During the summer of that year he traveled with a religious panorama. In 1876 he was elected a delegate to the republican national convention at Cincinnati and there voted for the nomination of Rutherford B. Hayes for president.

After the convention Mr. Burrus made an extensive tour throughout the North and East. On his return home he was chosen principal of the Yazoo city school at Yazoo, Miss. He subsequently taught two years in his Alma Mater College, the Fisk University, and received the degree of A. M. In 1879 he began reading law and was admitted to the bar in 1881. In 1883 he

PROF. JOHN H. BURRUS.

was selected for the presidency of the Alcorn Agricultural and Mechanical College at Rodney, Miss., which has grown to be one of the most important institutions of learning in the South under his administration. He is a gentleman of the finest culture, devoted to his profession, and highly esteemed throughout Mississippi by all classes of people.

Besides representing his people at the Cincinnati Convention in 1876 Prof. Burrus has been a good deal of a politician and has manifested an aptitude for public life. He was secretary of the Tennessee republican convention in 1878 and was secretary and treasurer of the State Executive Committee for two years. He was elected a school director at Nashville in 1878 and was re-elected in 1881, beating the combined vote of two competitors, one white man and one negro, although the majority of the people of the district were white. The other two directors were white men, yet Mr. Burrus was made chairman of the board and charged with the duty of visiting all the schools and seeing that the course of instruction was rigidly followed.

Since being placed at the head of the Alcorn University Prof. Burrus has abjured political life and proposes to devote the balance of his days strictly to educational interests. He has done much towards the elevation of his race. He does not believe in any man complaining that his color has kept him down in life. He believes that brains and character will always win. He has scarcely yet reached the prime of life, and there is a prospect of his accomplishing a glorious work in the future.

WILEY JONES.

Among the successful ex-slaves the name of Wiley Jones, of Arkansas, shines with resplendent luster. All success is the result of innate qualities which mark and make a man. In a pecuniary sense Mr. Jones has met with unbounded success, and he certainly deserves the good fortune which has attended his labors since he was released from bondage.

Wiley Jones is a native of Georgia, having been born in Madison county, July 14, 1848. His parents are dead. When only five years old he was taken to Arkansas by his master, whose name was Fitz Yell. As soon as he was old enough he was made a house-boy, and he also drove the family carriage. He continued in these lines of employment for two years or more. His master was an original union man and enlisted in the Federal army at the first opportunity. His slave, Wiley Jones, followed him, and he

WILEY JONES.

continued in camp until peace was proclaimed. He then went to Waco, Texas, and drove from Brazos river to San Antonio, hauling cotton to the frontier. He next returned to Arkansas and worked on a plantation for monthly wages. In 1881 he went into the tobacco and cigar trade, in which business he rapidly accumulated a fortune. He is naturally a shrewd trader, and to his natural quickness of perception he is indebted for his business success, for he never had the advantage of a system of schooling, and hence his education is very limited, being such as he has picked up in life, as he came in contact with men and events. The school of adversity and experience is often the best teacher of men, especially of the class of persons who never yield to discouragement in life.

Mr. Jones is now a resident of Pine Bluff, one of the rapidly developing cities of the state of Arkansas. He has extended his business by securing the street car charter for that thriving place, and he has placed his car lines under thorough equipment. He is also treasurer of the Industrial Fair Association. He is the sole owner of the grounds whereon the fair has been held, and of the race track and park, which covers fifty-five acres of ground lying one mile distant from the main street of the city. The street car stables are also located on this tract.

In his mercantile business Mr. Jones carries a stock of goods valued at $15,000, and he estimates his total possessions at $125,000, which is augmenting at a rapid rate. In all probability the day is near at hand when he will be accounted a millionaire. He is also a great fancier of blooded stock, and owns a herd of Durham and Holstein cattle. He is likewise engaged in breeding fine trotting stock, and one of his stallions, "Executor," has a record of 2:21. On his farm he has about a dozen choice bred mares, and he keeps a professional driver to handle them, which insures the best of care and a fine development of speed.

Taken altogether, Wiley Jones may be regarded as one of the most successful business men of the country. It is only about a quarter of a century since he was emancipated from the bondage of slavery, and his advancement since that time has been prodigious. He is regarded as the soul of honor by his white neighbors, who esteem him as a gentleman of the first-class. He is liberal, charitable and humane, as well as enterprising and successful in business affairs.

JOHN WESLEY TERRY.

This gentleman is one of the natural mechanics of the land, who has raised himself from an humble origin to an honored position in the street railway service of a great city. He was born in Murray county, Tennessee, in the year 1846, and was the slave of one William Pickard until released from bondage by the circumstances of the rebellion. His earliest recollections are of a very crude nature. His mother was a field hand and was obliged to work on the farm the live-long day. Having no other resource, the subject of this sketch and an older brother, when but prattling infants, were placed in a pen every morning, with a sufficiency of food and water to answer their daily necessities, and left to their own resources until the tired mother returned from her daily toil to her cabin and her infant children. Truly this was a hard beginning of an humble life to produce the grand results which have followed in the years of manhood.

When the union armies entered Columbia, Tennessee, in the summer of 1863, the mother of Mr. Terry took her children and started for the Federal lines. She was received and cared for, and for a season was offered protection. The elder son, Henry, was old enough to bear arms, and enlisted in the union service. In time a change of commanders occurred at Columbia, and one Col. Myers assumed control of the place. He made it a rule to return all slaves to their masters when claimed. Accordingly Mrs. Terry and her younger son were sent back to Murray county. Arrived there the young man declared his emancipation to his former master, and threatened to report him to the union commander at the adjacent town for harboring and feeding rebel soldiers, that county having been occupied by union troops during their absence at Columbia. His old master begged him not to make such a report, promised to recognize his freedom and pay him wages for future service. Accordingly young Terry worked for two years as a farm hand for the man who had formerly been his lawful master.

In 1866 young Wesley went to Nashville to look for his mother, who had made a second attempt at escape from bondage. Having found her, he began the business of steamboating, while his mother kept house for him. In 1875 he went to Chicago and entered the employ of the West Division Street Car Company and worked for the corporation two years. He then went to Washington, D. C., and entered the Wayland Seminary, where he remained four years. He completed the normal course and then took a theological course, with a view of entering the ministry of the Baptist church, of which he was a member. But having contracted some debts during his collegiate course, he concluded to resume work in the car shops, where he has continued to the present time. In the course of a year he was made foreman, and has a large force of mechanics under his direction, he being the only man of color in the company's employment. He is highly respected by the officers of the company, and by the men who work under him. His skill as a machinist is of the highest order. He is a member of the Knights of Labor and a director of the Central Park Building and Loan association.

From a plantation hand in Tennessee this young man has risen to affluence and respectability. The progress of the ex-slave appears to be onward and upward.

P. B. S. PINCHBACK.

Few men in the South have attracted so large a share of public attention since the days of emancipation as the Hon. Pinckney Benton Stewart Pinchback, of New Orleans. He was born in Holmes County, Miss., May 10, 1837. He was the son of Major William Pinchback and a slave mother of mixed blood, Eliza Stewart, who claimed to have both Negro and Indian blood in her veins. Major Pinchback manumitted the girl Eliza Stewart, who bore him ten children, so it can scarcely be said that Gov. Pinchback ever was a slave, though the son of a slave mother. He is the sole survivor of the large family. The mother lived to a ripe old age, dying in 1884.

In 1846 young Pinchback with an elder brother was sent to Cincinnati to Gilmore's High School where they remained two years. On their return home they found Major Pinchback on his dying bed. The mother with five children hurried back to Cincinnati after the funeral in order to prevent the enslavement of the children by the white heirs of Major Pinchback's estate. While there the oldest son lost his mind. This calamity left the care of the family upon the subject of this sketch. He was then only twelve years old. He obtained work as a cabin boy on a canal boat at eight dollars a month, on the Miami canal, between Cincinnati and Toledo. He followed the canal for several years, on the Miami canal and on the Wabash and Erie canal in Indiana, for some time making his home at Terre Haute. From 1854 to 1861 he took to the business of steamboating on the Missouri, the Mississippi, the Red and the Yazoo rivers, rising to the dignity of

P. B. S. PINCHBACK.

a steward, which was the highest position a colored man could command in those days.

The career of Mr. Pinchback as a steamboat steward was brought to a termination by the outbreak of the civil war in 1861. The day he was 25 years old, May 10, 1862, he abandoned the steamboat Alonzo Childs at Yazoo City, Miss., ran the confederate blockade and arrived in New Orleans. He had scarcely arrived there before he had a difficulty with his brother-in-law, who was wounded in the affray. He was arrested on civil process and gave bail. Before his case came on for trial he was again arrested by the military, tried by court martial and committed to a term of two years in the workhouse on a charge of assault with intent to murder. He was committed to the workhouse May 25, 1862, but was released August 18 of the same year in order that he might enlist in the First Louisiana Volunteer Infantry, his enlistment being the condition of his release.

Soon after entering the military service Gen. B. F. Butler, then in command at New Orleans, issued his order calling upon the free men of color in the Crescent City to take up arms in defense of the union. Mr. Pinchback was made a recruiting sergeant and he opened an office for the enlistment of colored soldiers. On the 12th of October the Second Regiment of the Louisiana Native Guards was mustered into service with Captain P. B. S. Pinchback in command of Company A. His career in the army was brief but stormy. He strove to maintain his own dignity and the rights of the troops under his command. The Federal soldiers were as hostile to the black troops as the most belligerent rebels. Capt. Pinchback was in hot water all the time. He was in constant trouble with the street car officials, who ejected him time and again. He also had a difficulty with the colonel of his regiment, whom he accused of mistreating his men. His troubles came so thick and fast that September 3, 1863, he tendered his resignation and it was accepted.

But Capt. Pinchback could not be idle. He soon sought an interview with Gen. N. P. Banks, who succeeded Gen. Butler. The General was favorably impressed and issued an order permitting Capt. Pinchback to recruit a company of colored cavalry. The company was raised but a commission was refused to Pinchback because of his color. This act of injustice closed his military career. He did not again seek to serve his country as a soldier.

Mr. Pinchback soon turned his attention to political affairs. In the fall of 1865 he spoke in Mobile, Montgomery, and Selma, Alabama, denouncing the unjust treatment which the colored people were receiving at the hands of lawless and vicious men. April 9, 1867 he organized the Fourth Ward Republican Club in New Orleans, and he was elected a member of the republican state committee, a position he has occupied almost continuously since that time. He was appointed a commissioner of customs by Hon. Wm. Pitt Kellogg, May 22, 1867, Mr. Kellogg being collector of the port at that time. He, however, declined the position to become a candidate for a seat in the constitutional convention then about to be held. He was elected and was a leading member of the convention. He reported the civil rights article guaranteeing equality to all the citizens of the state. At the first election under the new constitution he was elected a state senator. In 1868 he was chosen a delegate-at-large to the Chicago convention which nominated Gen. Grant for the presidency.

The next year he entered into business and established the commission and cotton factorage house of Pinchback and Antoine. The firm did an immense business and had Mr. Pinchback kept out of politics, he would probably have become one of the wealthiest men in the world in a very short time. As it was he accumulated a handsome fortune.

In December, 1870, Mr. Pinchback engaged in the publication of the New Orleans Louisianian, which he continued about eleven years. It was the organ of the colored race. The same year he endeavored to organize a Mississippi river packet company but did not meet with sufficient encouragement and he abandoned the enterprise. December 6, 1871, he was elected president protem of the state senate to fill the vacancy occasioned by the death of Hon. Oscar J. Dunn, and became the Acting Lieutenant Governor of the state. The next year he was nominated as the republican candidate for governor. The federal office holders had previously nominated Wm. Pitt Kellogg for that office. There was also a democratic ticket in the field, which was certain of success unless a compromise could be made between the two wings of the republican party. Such a compromise was finally arranged and Kellogg was made governor while Pinchback was elected congressman-at-large; and the success of this mutual arrangement probably had the effect of continuing republican supremacy in Louisiana for three or four years. But there was a factional fight raging inside of the republican ranks, which could not fail to injure party domination in the

long run, and it seriously impaired the hope of Governor Pinchback continuing in the same prominence he had occupied since the
close of the war.   Governor Warmoth espoused the cause of
Horace Greeley, and for a time acted with the democratic party.
When the legislature convened Governor Pinchback was chosen
United States senator, but the Warmoth republicans refused to
vote for him, and although he was declared elected and received a
certificate, there was so much doubt surrounding the case that the
Federal senate refused to seat him.   After a continued reference
for three years, to the senatorial committee on elections, the right
of Governor Pinchback to be sworn as a member was denied by a
vote of 29 ayes and 32 noes.   This contest was a very remarkable
one.   There was no other claimant for the vacant seat, and Gov.
Pinchback was armed with full credentials for the place he sought,
but his right to a seat was finally denied.   While this long contest was pending the term of congress, to which Gov. Pinchback
was elected as a member at large to the house of representatives,
expired.   The very remarkable · picture was presented in this
instance of a man holding certificates of election to both houses of
congress, and though asking admission, he was not accepted in
either house.

    When the political troubles came on in Louisiana which fol-
lowed the appointment of the National Electoral Commission, in
1877, Governor Pinchback managed to pay off some of his political
debts.   He was instrumental in having the Nicholls state government recognized, although the electoral vote of the state was
counted for Mr. Hayes, while S. B. Packard, the republican candidate for governor against General Nicholls, had more votes in the
state than were cast for the Hayes and Wheeler electoral ticket.

    The political asperities existing within the republican party of
Louisiana, measurably died away after the state passed under democratic control.   One of the earliest acts of the administration of
Governor Nicholls was to appoint Mr. Pinchback a member of the
State Board of Education, a position he had already held with
acceptability for six years.   He was appointed an internal revenue
agent March 5, 1879, and held the office until he was elected, from
Madison Parish, to a seat in the convention called to remodel the
first reconstruction constitution of Louisiana.   He was a delegate at
large to the Chicago convention of 1880, which nominated Garfield
and Arthur, and when General Arthur became President after
Guiteau's assassination of President Garfield, he appointed Governor Pinchback to the office of collector at New Orleans.

Although advanced in years beyond the ordinary life of students, Governor Pinchback entered the law school of the State University of Louisiana, in 1885, and April 10, 1886, he was admitted to the bar in the city of New Orleans, just one month before he was forty-nine years old. It is not often that a man passes through nearly a half century of existence before he makes application for admission to the bar in the courts of a great city, but it must be borne in mind that Governor Pinckney B. S. Pinchback is a very wonderful man. He would succeed where thousands of others fail.

Governor Pinchback is in the enjoyment of a large legal practice and is coining money. He is wealthy. There are few men of larger liberality than he. The vicissitudes of his life have been such as attach to the fortunes of very few men. Of large brain, of large heart and broad views, Governor Pinchback is a man to make himself felt wherever his future lines may be cast. He belongs to a race of men who could not be otherwise than aggressive, but his aggressions have always been found earnest, and honest, as the seeming right commanded the approbation of his judgment. The future of Governor Pinchback will likely be found as interesting as his past, if circumstances shall again call him into the seething turmoil of public strife.

BLANCHE K. BRUCE.

Here we have a man with a woman's name. He might as well have been named Mary or Jane as Blanche; but his mother gave him the name and that is all we know about it. He bears it worthily and well.

Blanche K. Bruce was born in Virginia, March 1, 1841. His parents were slaves, and he was born in bondage. In his early days his mother removed to St. Louis and he grew nearly to manhood in that city. While there, a little barefoot, ragged urchin, peddling newspapers on the levee, he was one day accosted by a gentleman who was hastily making his way down the levee, enroute to a steamboat which was nearly ready to pull out upon its destination for the lower Mississippi river, with:

"Here, you damned little nigger, take this satchel and carry it aboard that steamboat," pointing to it, "or I'll throw you in the river."

The boy took a package, nearly as big as himself, and hurried upon the steamboat. The owner of the luggage came aboard just as the stage-plank was being pulled upon deck, and the "damned little nigger" had to hustle ashore without getting one cent for his service as a carrier.

BLANCHE K. BRUCE.

Years passsed by, and the owner of the satchel was a member of the United States Senate, from the great State of Missouri. His name was Lewis V. Bogy (pronounced Bozhee, with accent on the second syllable). While Mr. Bogy was a senator, Mr. Bruce was made a member of the senate from Mississippi. The Missouri senator had a bill pending which was of local importance. He went to Mr. Bruce, explained its importance, and solicited his vote. The colored man promptly responded that he would vote for the bill. He then proceeded :   •

"Senator Bogy, do you remember a little ragged negro that carried your carpet-bag to a steamboat, years ago, at the St. Louis levee and only received a few divine curses for his service?"

"Yes;" said Mr. Bogy, "what of it?"

"Why, I am that contemptible little nigger," said Senator Bruce, "and you owe me for that service yet. Of course I will vote for your bill."

Senator Bogy hastily made a computation of the value of that service with compound interest and tendered payment, which was promptly refused. The twain, however, repaired to the senate restaurant and "smiled." Bogy and Bruce remained firm friends until the death of the former.

After the war of negro independence Mr. Bruce entered Oberlin college, and took an elective course. His association with young gentlemen of general intelligence awakened a dormant thirst for knowledge and the practical application of scholarly information.

He migrated to Mississippi after the war and began life as a planter, believing that to be his vocation in life. In 1868 he took an active part in political affairs. Two years later he was sergeant-at-arms of the Mississippi senate, and while in that capacity was thrown in active contact with the best men of the state. He filled the office of assessor for his county, and was subsequently made sheriff. Then he was chosen a member of the Board of Levee Commissioners for the Mississippi river.

In 1874, Mr. Bruce was made a senator of the United States from Mississippi. He served a full term. During his senatorial career he was the friend of Roscoe Conkling, who conducted him to the bar of the senate when he was first sworn into office. He was made register of the treasury under the regime of Mr. Garfield and is to-day doing a pension business in Washington. Blanche K. Bruce is a big man every way.

THE COLORED MINISTRY.

In presenting a few sketches of the success in life that has attended former slaves, after being released from bondage, it is appropriate that honorable mention should be made of men who have devoutly stepped into the sacred desk and labored with zeal and efficiency for the benefit, temporal and eternal, of their fellow-men. In doing so it is fair to say the writer thinks there must be intense disgust in the minds of honorable people at the expression of Booker T. Washington, a colored man, holding the honorable position of president of the Tuskegee Normal School, in a communication which he furnished to the *Christian Union*. After stating that three-fourths of the Baptist ministers and two-thirds of the Methodist " are unfit, either mentally or morally or both, to preach the Gospel to anyone or to lead anyone," the honorable professor subsides into flippancy and says:

The character of many of these preachers can be judged by one, of whom it was said that while he was at work in a cotton field, in the middle of July, he suddenly stopped, looked upward and said : " Oh, Lord, de work is so hard, de cotton is so grassy, an' de sun am so hot — I belive dis darkey am called to preach." With few exceptions the preaching of the colored ministry is emotional in the highest degree, and the minister considers himself successful in proportion as he is able to set the people in all parts of the congregation to groaning, uttering wild screams, and jumping, and finally going into a trance.. One of the principal ends sought by most of these ministers is their salary, and to this everything else is made subservient.

It may be feared that many white ministers, highly educated and very devoted to the work of human salvation, have an eye to their salaries as the chief end of man; and they make everything else subservient to a payment into the treasury of the Lord, for the behoof of the educated ministry, of a sum of money that will make them independent when they grow old and are " retired " by the order of the congress of the church. Very few — ah, how few — of the educated white divines of the day surrender a fat living to go into the wilderness and preach for a bare subsistence! The number of men who have done this thing, under the call of Jehovah, are scarcer than hen's teeth, of mythical anatomy. Ye proud divines, who condemn the service of colored ministers, are no better than they. Everyone of you work for pay, and you would be driving wagons, in all probability, in case your churches should sit down upon your ministration. There is not, in all the United States, a more devout set of churchmen than the colored ministers of the

South, who preach the Gospel to men of their color as best they
know how, for a bare subsistence. They follow the calling of the
Master, in spirit and in truth. The highest realm of the churches
would be glad to welcome them in the pulpit, *except for their
color!*

History does not tell us the color of the humble fishermen, called in the name of Jesus, when he planned the way of universal salvation. It is scarcely probable that any of them were of the classes
from whence the nations of the north spread over the barren soil
of Europe, and finally adventured to America, perhaps before the
discoveries of Columbus. The followers of the meek and lowly
Savior belonged to the southern climes of Europe and Asia. They
were of the classes of men to whom Christ gave the edict "Go
ye into all the world and preach the Gospel to every creature."
When he sent them forth he gave them a line of service which the
white men of to-day have failed to follow. He said: "Provide
neither gold nor silver nor brass in your purses. Nor scrip for
your journey, neither two coats, neither shoes nor yet staves; for
the workman is worthy of his meat."

If the churchmen of to-day were required, at final judgment,
to conform to the edict of the Great Master, it is to be feared that
the bottomless pit would be inhabited by whites and blacks in proportion to their numerical order, without reference to their means
of education. Educational lines would be a reproach to the white
race. Then the golden rule might be amended to read: "Do unto
others as ye have done unto them."

REV. HARVEY JOHNSON.

In Fauquier county, Virginia, August 4, 1843, Harvey
Johnson entered upon existence, the son of slave parents. He
happened to belong to a class of people willing to accord to their
servants an exercise of religious freedom, even though they were
unable to enjoy personal freedom. He remained in slavery until
the days of the war, and when federal troops took possession of
the surroundings of Washington, Mr. Johnson found no difficulty
in going within the union lines, where he had the protection of
the federal troops. Afterwards he took a course of study at the
Wayland seminary, in the city of Washington, supported by anti-
slavery friends. In 1872 he began to preach, and in the fall of
that year he was called to the Union Baptist church at Baltimore,
Maryland. He occupies the pulpit of that church to-day. He is
an educated minister of the gospel, has an interesting family, and

REV. HARVEY JOHNSON.

he is exerting his utmost efforts to promote the negro race in the
social and religious scale.

Mr. Johnson is in no sense a politician. His professional work
occupies his whole time, coupled with a devoted interest in the
cause of education. He is doing all that his soul and body can
endure to make his people known and honored among men. His
logic, his eloquence and his devout spirit, would introduce life
into many a white congregation, provided he could spread a
mask over his facial anatomy and pose before the people as a fair
skinned person. Verily, the face of the Lord in eclipse is antago-
nistic to the accomplishment of the salvation of souls. The loyal
white element is not disposed to trend unto salvation by the side
of the negro who has faith in God.

REV. PROFESSOR HOLMES.

In contradistinction to most of the people of the black race,
who started in life under adverse circumstances, Prof. Holmes is
an example of the fact that many southern masters were just and
humane. He is still a young man, comparatively speaking, and
will probably be able to do much for the advancement of his race
before he ceases his life of labor and devotion to the cause of his
people. It has been a favorite theory since the war to represent
the southern people as brutal and inhuman in the treatment of
their slaves, but Prof. Holmes is a living example of the fact that
many educated men of the African race will voluntarily stand up
and testify to the contrary.

William E. Holmes was born at Augusta, Georgia, January
22, 1856. He was a slave. His father belonged to one master
and his mother to another. They lived for a while on adjacent
plantations and were not forbidden family privileges. Their
association was harmonious, and their social relations were not
disturbed until the mother of Holmes was hired abroad to a con-
tracting carpenter, a man of generous feelings and impulses, who
gave her large personal liberty. The carpenter took a liking to
the son of his hired employe and made him a favorite. He went
with his master in all his travels, and had a bed in the family
mansion as well as a place at the family table. Still the master was
not in favor of the abolition of involuntary slavery.

Mr. Holmes had the advantage of books and papers, and at
an early age became a fair scholar. After the close of the war the
devoted mother gave her son the advantage of good instruction from 1865 to 1871. He became a proficient scholar.

Having united with the Baptist church, Mr. Holmes renewed his studies at the Augusta Institute and the Atlanta Seminary, where he graduated in 1881. He had already been ordained to preach, but he continued his studies at Yale University for two years, making a specialty of the study of the Hebrew language. He was made corresponding secretary of the Missionary Baptist convention of Georgia in May, 1883, and since that date he has wrought earnestly for the upbuilding of his church and his race in the South. He is recognized as a ripe scholar, a deep thinker, and his lectures have received a wide admiration.

Prof. Holmes is a truly pious man, a scholar and a worker. He does not make his labor a specialty for his race, but takes in his line of study and assistance all the men of the world. His heart is as big as the universe though his color is black. May God give to the world many men like Prof. Holmes.

REV. R. B. VANDERVALL.

This gentleman first saw the light of day near Nesley's Bend, on the Tennessee river, about ten miles above the city of Nashville. His father was a Virginia slave, owned by a man named Carroll Foster. His mother was a slave woman, the property of one Major Hall, who emigrated from Virginia to Tennessee and settled about ten miles above the city of Nashville. The Rev. Dr. Vandervall is now about 59 years old.

When seven years old the little boy Vandervall was hired out at public sale, on New Year's day, pursuant to a statute then prevailing in Tennessee. He had never lived in a white family, and when an old man came to him saying, "Come with me," the boy was badly frightened. He was snatched from his mother's arms, placed on a horse bare-back and made to ride twenty-two miles across the country. He was thus ruthlessly cut loose from all the dear ties of earth.

In his new abode the poor boy, who had neither home nor name, was made to sleep at night rolled up in a piece of rag carpet, where he cried himself to sleep night after night. In time he became accommodated to his situation. He slept in the house with the white family, and repeated the prayer nightly taught by his slave mother. He enjoyed one privilege—he was allowed to attend school.

When ten years old the poor boy was taken to Nashville, where he was hired to a minister of the gospel named Garrett. While residing there the estate of his old master, who had died, was par-

REV. R. B. VANDEWALL.

titioned. He was purchased by Mr. Vandervall, whose name he continues to bear.

John Vandervall, the son of the master, took a liking to the lad and continued the instruction that had been begun by Mr. Garrett. He had a religious turn of mind and attended weekly prayer meetings, where he prayed and began to exhort. He took a wife and began to ,work on a railroad, so that he might pass a part of his time with his companion in the journey of life, but his master found that he could read and write, and feared his intelligence. He threatened to sell him south. The consequence was the young man ran away. He afterwards returned home and was hired to a man at Nashville on his own terms, paying his master $200 a year for the privilege.

About this time Mr. Vandervall had a queer dream. He thought he was sold to a cotton planter, and, fearing that the dream would come to a reality, he made a proposition to his master for his own purchase. The offer was accepted, and he paid a stipulated sum every year. When he had paid $500 his master made a bargain to sell him into Texas. He ran away a second time.

This time friends intervened and the money for his purchase was paid. He took the advantage of his freedom, educated himself and began to preach. He afterward undertook the purchase of his wife, and had made the last annual payment for her liberty when the civil war broke out, which would have given her freedom.

Perhaps the most remarkable instance of delivery from servitude is to be found in the case of Dr. Vandervall. After the war he settled in East Tennessee and took a lively interest in the education of his race. He continued his own culture and has taken high rank in the institutions of the South for the education of the colored race. He has earned and received several educational degrees. Mr. Vandervall has two sons who are ripe scholars.

The case of this noble gentleman of color affords a notable instance of success under difficulties. If ever a pension was deserved it is in his case. He is to-day modestly pursuing the avocation of a cultured Christian minister.

JOHN R. LYNCH.

The history of the negro race abounds with cultured orators whose electricity has astonished the world. Among those who have established a name and a fame within the United States, no man is entitled to prominence above that of John R. Lynch.

The south has produced a colored citizen, in the person of Mr. Lynch, who has maintained his manhood, to the honor of his race and his own place in history.

John R. Lynch was born in Concordia parish, Louisiana, September 10, 1847. He was a slave and continued in the life of a slave until he was freed by the acts of emancipation. He had no education in early life, and emerged from the reign of despotism in utter ignorance of the qualities God had given him. But the light cannot be hidden completely, even when it is under a bushel measure. In the face of his training as a field hand, Mr. Lynch has risen to eminence, and is to-day recognized as a power within the land.

When the union troops took possession of the city of Natchez, his mother, who had saved some means, gave her son the benefit of private instruction. He made himself acquainted with the written history of ancient and modern times. His first venture in business was in photography. While operating a gallery in Natchez Gov. Ames appointed him a justice of the peace at Natchez. In the fall of 1869 he was elected to the legislature of Mississippi. He was re-elected in 1871, and was made speaker of the house of representatives near the close of the session. From the state legislature he was made a member of congress, and served in the Forty-third and Forty-fourth congresses. He was again elected, fairly, to the Forty-seventh congress, and contested the seat of the despicable General Chalmers, of infamous Fort Pillow memory.

While awaiting a report of his case on the part of the house committee on privileges and elections for the Forty-seventh congress, Mr. Lynch was one day found walking along Pennsylvania avenue, of the city of Washington, by a gentleman who had frequently observed his familiar figure. He was hailed and this question asked of him:

"Can you tell me, my man, where I can find a competent carriage driver? I prefer a colored man."

Mr. Lynch said he was not aware of any person needing such employment, but there were doubtless many such, and he promised to make inquiry, at the same time making a note of the gentleman's name and address.

"You seem to be pretty well informed as to the localities of Washington and Georgetown, as I often see you moving around. Why cannot I employ you? Evidently you are out of a job. What are you doing anyhow?"

"You are right in saying I am out of a job just now," was
the reply of Mr. Lynch, "but I hope to have one pretty soon. I
am contesting the seat of Gen. Chalmers in congress and think I
am very liable to get it."

The inquirer looked at the negro in a surprised manner, and
then remarked: "I supposed I was talking to a 'nigger' and not
to a statesman. Times seem to have changed. Good day."

He walked off with a bug in his ear.

When the national republican convention met in Chicago in
1884, Mr. Lynch was made temporary chairman of that body,
beating Powell Clayton, ex-senator from Arkansas, for the honor.
He is the only negro who ever presided over a national convention of any party within the United States. His knowledge of
parliamentary law, acquired while speaker of the house of representatives of Mississippi, stood him in good place. He ruled
decorously, wisely and acceptably.

Mr. Lynch is married to a southern colored lady, and manages
a plantation in the vicinity of Natchez with credit and profit to
himself and family. He is moving quietly in private life, but is
likely to resume political life at any moment. He is respected
and honored by all who know him, whites and blacks alike.

JOHN M. LANGSTON.

There lives to-day at Petersburg, Va., a gentleman of distinction, though of negro blood, who deserves the high regard of his
countrymen who admire true greatness whether clothed in a white
or black skin.   John M. Langston was born in Louisa county,
Virginia, December 14, 1829.   He bears in his veins the blood of
three races of men — the negro, the Indian and the Anglo-Saxon;
but his mother was a slave and in pursuance of the edict of the
law made by white men he was born in slavery, although his
father was his master.   He bears the name of his father and dif-
fers from many of his fellow slaves of other days in this—that he
was not emancipated by circumstances growing out of the war of
the rebellion, but was made free by the last will and testament of
his master, and that instrument made provision for his education.
He does not, perhaps, fall within the classes designed to be supplied with a pension under the Vaughan ex-slave pension bill, but
he presents such an illustrious instance of great ability and force
of character, and as one of the men who have been ranked as
negroes, that it is meet and proper that he should receive an honorable mention among the noble men who have sought to raise the

black race to a position of deserved respect and prominence. On his mother's side Mr. Langston lays claim to the distinction of having descended from Pocahontas — a distinction that he divides with many high-born Virginia families.

Made free by virtue of his father's will, John M. Langston was sent in early life to Ohio with a view of receiving proper instruction. He was received as a student at Oberlin College in 1844 and graduated from that university in 1849. He was thus launched upon the sea of life a free man of liberal education fully thirteen years before Abraham Lincoln issued his first proclamation of emancipation. After his graduation at Oberlin Mr. Langston made application for admission to a law school at Ballston Spa, near Saratoga, managed by Prof. J. W. Fowler. He was denied admission *on account of his color!* Inasmuch as his facial appearance and other prominent features did not mark his origin, he was advised by friends to claim that he was a Spaniard, hailing from the West Indies or South America, so that he might secure matriculation in the law school. But his better judgment rebelled against any attempt at deception. Mr. Langston turned away from Ballston with a sad heart in order that he might try his fortunes elsewhere. He met with another rebuff at the Cincinnati law school, and then concluded to read law in the office of some private instructor. But in this field of learning he met with scarcely better success.

After repeated failure to secure a student's place in a private law office, Mr. Langston obtained the loan of some elementary works from the library of Hon. Sherlock J. Andrews, of Cleveland, and began a system of self-instruction, receiving occasional suggestions from and making recitations to his preceptor. But this method of instruction was so unsatisfactory and was attended with so many difficulties that Mr. Langston finally concluded to abandon the law. He returned to his old *alma mater* at Oberlin and took a theological course, graduating in that department in 1853. But his heart was set upon a legal education; and he finally effected an arrangement whereby he entered the law office of Hon. Philemon Bliss, at Elyria, Ohio, where he devoted himself to the study of law with singular assiduity. In the course of twelve months Mr. Langston made application for admission to practice in the local courts. The presiding judge selected a committee for his examination consisting of one whig and two democratic attorneys. The committee was sensibly impressed with Mr. Langston's profound and varied learning, his elementary knowledge of the law being perfect and his general knowledge equal to that of a belles-lettres scholar. His admittance to the bar was recommended, but here the color line was struck to his discomfiture, the question of the right of a court to give a certificate to a negro having been raised. About this time, however, the supreme court of Ohio decided, in an election contest, the term "negro or mulatto" in the state constitution meant a preponderance of white or black blood. In the case of Mr. Langston it was readily shown that the preponderance of blood in his veins was white, and thereupon the local court made an order that he be sworn as an attorney. He was admitted to the bar October 24, 1854. It is doubtful whether any learned lawyer ever had greater difficulties in securing admission to practice before the civil courts than those which environed Mr. Langston in the early part of his career.

After his admission to the bar, Mr. Langston settled at Brownhelm, Lorain county, Ohio, upon a farm, but within a brief time was associated with Mr. Hamilton Perry, a profound lawyer, in the trial of a cause involving the title to lands. There were no colored people in the vicinity. The court, jurors, witnesses and other attorneys in the case were white men. Mr. Perry purposely entrusted the management of the cause to his associate, reserving to himself only the place of a consulting counsel. The trial of a case by a negro lawyer excited widespread local comment and the court was filled with spectators. The result of the trial was a sweeping victory for John M. Langston. Thereafter his fortune was made. Business flowed in upon him, and he had a larger practice than he was able to accommodate.

Mr. Langston's first appearance as an orator in the political field occurred in 1865. His reputation as a lawyer had been so great that he was invited to attend and address the May meeting of the American Anti-Slavery Society, in that year, at the City of New York. His address was cultured and his eloquence magnetic. At the age of 36 years he found himself with a national reputation, and his name associated with that aggressive line of heroes whose mission was the destruction of African slavery within the United States.

For several years Mr. Langston was intimately connected with the cause of education in the State of Ohio, and gave special attention to the organization of schools for the education of the colored youth of that great state. He held the office of a school visitor by appointment, and he traversed from the lakes to the Ohio river, organizing schools wherever they were required and secured **for**

them a supply of teachers. He was engaged in this work when the
war broke out in 1861. He immediately added to his efforts the
patriotic work of encouraging enlistments for service in the field.
He was instrumental in recruiting the 54th and 55th regiments of
Ohio infantry, and after the enlistment of colored troops was permitted he recruited the 5th colored regiment, to which he presented
a stand of colors. He visited Washington and asked of Secretary
Stanton the privilege of recruiting a colored regiment to be officered by colored men. His project was endorsed and supported
by the late James A. Garfield, but was not decided in time to enable him to participate personally in the acts of the war. After
the war had concluded, in 1867, President Johnson appointed Mr.
Langston minister to Hayti, but he did not accept the office. The
same year, on motion of Mr. Garfield, he was admitted to practice
law before the Supreme Court of the United States. He was at
that time actively engaged in the organization of freedmen's
schools under the appointment and instruction of General O. O.
Howard, and he deemed the work of such importance that he would
not leave it to go abroad. In this field of labor he continued until
1869, when was called to the professorship of law in the Howard
University. He was made dean of the department and gave seven
of the best years of his life to the up-building of that institution. The college has graduated many able law students, white
and colored, male and female. During two years of his connection
with the college he was its vice-president and president. The
degree of L.L. D. was conferred upon him, marked by an impressive
address from Gen. Howard.

During the administration of President Grant, it was his pleasure to name Mr. Langston as a member of the board of health of
the District of Columbia, and he served six years or more, as the
attorney of the board, and a part of the time as its secretary. In
1877 President Hayes appointed him minister resident, and consul
general to Hayti, about ten years after he had declined a similar
position under Andrew Johnson. This time he accepted and for
about eight years did excellent and valuable service in his diplomatic relations. He was very popular at the Haytien Court, and
stood high with the representatives of all governments represented
in that republic.

In January, 1885, Mr. Langston resigned his foreign appointment and returned home the following summer, intending to
resume the practice of his profession. He found, however, that he
had been chosen, by the board of education of Virginia, president

of the Virginia Normal School and Collegiate Institute, and a large annual appropriation was made for the maintenance of the institution. His success in managing this great university has been phenomenal, and has called forth the highest enconiums of those associated with him, and of the state officers of Virginia.

In 1888 Mr. Langston was induced, much against his will, to accept a nomination for congress in the Petersburg district and would have unquestionably have been elected by a large majority but for the antipathy of the friends of Gen. Mahone, who induced Mr. R. W. Arnold to run as an independent republican candidate against him. According to the official returns Mr. E. C. Venable (dem.) received 13,299 votes in the district ; Mr. John M. Langston (regular rep.) received 12,657 votes, and Mr. R. W. Arnold (ind. rep.) received 3,207 votes. For reasons not necessary here to state, Mr. Langston contested the seat of Mr. Venable, and the contest was decided in Mr. Langston's favor September 23, 1890. It is understood that Mr. Langston's contest was impeded by the active opposition of Gen. Mahone and his friends.

Among the men who have risen from the cradle of slavery to eminence none stand higher than Mr. Langston. He is a noble product of our free and liberal institutions. There is a brilliant life yet awaiting him.

CONCLUSION OF SKETCHES.

It would be impracticable, in the space allotted to a volume like the one in hand, to include even a brief sketch of the many distinguished descendants of African parents, who have been born in slavery but who have carved for themselves an enduring reputation in subsequent lives of honor and successful struggle against the untoward circumstances of their birth. It would be a pleasure to narrate the achievements of such a man as the Rev. W. J. Simmons, who distinguished himself as a Christian minister and a man of letters. While discharging the duties of the presidency of the State University at Louisville, Ky., Dr. Simmons wrote and published a volume entitled "Men of Mark : Eminent, Progressive and Rising," which is almost invaluable as a delineation of those negro men of ability who have honored their race in every department of life. There have been very many others who have emerged from the barbarism of slavery, and through trials and dangers, equal to the sufferings of the children of Israel during their forty years of wanderings in desert and wilderness, they have come forth at last to benefit the human race. It may seem unfair to omit honorable mention of any of them, put the purpose in view is not to praise, but to make a plea for justice, long delayed, and in doing so to satisfy the general reader that the sons of slavery have earned a recognition in the lives and services of those of their number who have been able to outgrow the conditions surrounding their birth, and to become useful to the world in their day and generation.

Perhaps it may be said that the writer of these pages has singled out a few illustrious examples, and that comparatively few negroes could, under any circumstances, cope with Dr. Simmons, Frederick Douglass, John M. Langston, John R. Lynch, Robert B. Elliott, Robert Smalls, Samuel R. Lowery, John Wesley Terry and others, some of whom have been biographically sketched in these pages, while it has not been convenient to make creditable mention of all of them. Such, indeed, may be the fact. It would possibly be right to go one step farther, and to say that even the advantages of learning and fortune would not fit all negroes to rank with the men whose names have been mentioned. But because all of the dusky race cannot rise to eminence in the learned professions, in skilled trades or in the strife of arms, it does not follow that a great nation should refuse to those of the race a proper recognition for their lives of toil who have been held in bondage for years, and even for generations, and who have finally been turned loose by that nation to starve and die without any resources whatever.

Those captious critics who would suffer the ex-slaves to look upon their freedom from involuntary servitude as a full and complete recompense for their former years of captivity, because all of them have not shown their capacity to become statesmen and scholars, are reminded that comparatively few white men, though free from birth, have been able to claim a rank with Washington, Jefferson, Madison, Clay, Webster, Calhoun, Irving, Bryant, Longfellow, Bancroft, Whittier and hundreds more, living and dead, who have given renown to our country in statesmanship, literature, science and arms. Yet courts, congress and legislatures have always been ready to award a full measure of damages to white men who have suffered wrong in any way at the hands of the nation, the states or the people. Only in the case of the negro do we find an indisposition to right a wrong that has followed the sad fortunes of that race from the time when their forefathers were dragged unwilling captives to American soil and loaded down with the galling chains of slavery. The error is as old as the government—yea, older than that—it began with the discovery of the western hemisphere and has continued unto the present day, in spite of the work of emancipation which bade the black man lift up his head and snuff the air of liberty as the natural right of man. But liberty without compensation for the long era of slavish toil is but a mockery of justice.

In how many instances has the book of time recorded the fact that some poor mortal has been made the victim of a chain of circumstances which dragged him from his home to become the inmate of a prison cell? In the lapse of time his innocence was established. The state made haste to unbar the prison doors and set the victim free. In all such cases a reparation for the wrong of imprisonment has been made from the public treasury. And the money value, fixed as a recompense for the years of anguish, torture and imprisonment, has been gauged by a liberal if not a lavish hand. It was due to the victim of the law's mistake, that he should be treated with a generosity commensurate with the injustice he suffered on the part of the state when it laid its hand upon him in error and branded him as a felon stained with crime.

If the state stands ready to offer liberal remuneration to the citizen who has suffered a term of imprisonment in obedience to an error of a court of justice, how much the more ready should a great government always be to repair its error in holding a countless class of its subjects in the horrors of vassalage during generation after generation of mankind? In the one case the prisoner was suspected of a crime which subsequent events demonstrated he did not commit. In the other case there was not even an unjust suspicion of wrong-doing upon which the torture of captivity could be exercised. The misfortune of caste alone served the purpose of burning the brand of slavery upon the backs of myriads of human beings. Might was law and right was not recognized. The toil, the sweat, the groans, the tears, and even the blessings of years of human slavery, stand up in a line together and appeal to the congress of the United States to be just to the injured men and women of the Negro race who have born the heat and burden of the era of slavery, and who have lost home and fireside in answer to a prayer for human freedom!

Incidental to the advancement made by former subjects of slavery, since the acquirement of their freedom, it may be stated that the free people of color within the United States have presented some notable examples of eminence in various departments of life; and the success of such persons has unquestionably wrought a wholesome influence upon the brightest of the negroes who emerged from slavery. Animated by the knowledge that persons of their own color had acquired property, in a measure that gave them prominence and respectability, the freedmen who were ambitious of making the most of their new condition, made haste to secure education and then to apply that education in a practical and beneficent manner. Of course the plea for a pension to be granted to the freedmen of the former slave states does not apply to those persons of color who have been free from their birth. But no class of men will rejoice more heartily than negroes who have never been slaves to see ample justice done to their fellow men who have endured the distress of slavery in former days. In the days of the great civil war, when the first gleam of the sunlight of liberty seemed about to pierce the black cloud of bondage, all over the North and in many parts of the South, the first rays of political independence were watched for eagerly and welcomed with glad alacrity by no association of men with the same solicitude that characterized the free men of color. While universal freedom would add nothing to their well-being, except to extend their lines of usefulness and to enable them to enter upon a larger arena in the pursuit of commercial and business avocations, they had that natural love and affection for the people of their race that their hearts swelled with feelings of gratitude, patriotism and true christian devotion at the prospect of personal liberty throughout the land to all the inhabitants thereof. And when at last the edict went forth which surrendered the shackles of nearly six millions of human beings into the giant grasp of Abraham Lincoln, the anthem of praise and the voice of thanksgiving swelled up from the hearts of the free men of color in every part of the land with an enthusiasm that bespoke them a happy people, devoutly thankful to Almighty God for the boundless favor of freedom to all mankind without regard to race, color or previous condition of bondage.

That the goodly example of the best element of the original free negro population has had much to do in the amelioration of the condition of the ex-slaves there can be no manner of doubt or question. The history of the United States abounds with the glorious work of such noble men of the African race as Rev. W. B. Derrick, D. D., Rev. James A. D. Pond (deceased), Rev. Theodore Doughty Miller, D. D., Rev. HenryW. Chandler, and many other christian ministers of the gospel; J. D. Baltimore who had a high reputation as a mechanical engineer; and a musical composer of the ability of Henry F. Williams; such distinguished lawyers as James

C. Matthews, who was Mr. Cleveland's register of deeds at Washington, Alexander Clark, Prof. T. McC. Stewart, and a score of others of the same profession, dozens of distinguished physicians, and hosts of the ablest teachers in the land. In proportion to their number it may be seriously questioned whether there can be found within the confines of this great American union of states a more talented body of men than the professional and scientific citizens of color who were free from their childhood. In the race of progress they have kept even with the rapid advance of civilization, and during the last quarter of a century they have stimulated manhood, education and social eminence among their brethren released from the thraldom of slavery. While not beneficiaries themselves of the proposed act for the pension of freedmen it is very certain that the ex-slaves will not rejoice more heartily than the free men of color over the passage of such a just and righteous statute.

It may be safely assumed that the more the proposition shall be discussed, to extend a just and equitable system of pensions to the persons who were restrained of their natural liberty during a large portion of their lives, the greater favor it will find with all rational and thinking men. It has been very justly remarked in moral philosophy that "there is no excellence without great labor." It may also be said that no reform was ever proposed in government without encountering the severest criticism and opposition of ignorance, as well as of that class of capitalists who berate any act of justice which is likely to call for an assessment for taxation upon their stores of wealth. It is to be expected that the proposition to pension ex-slaves of this Republic will call forth bitter opposition, intense efforts at ridicule and sarcasm, and in many instances the most disgusting ribaldry and even obscenity. In truth the work of misrepresentation and detraction has actually begun.

Such newspapers as the Chicago *Herald*, the Nashville *American*, and the Cleveland *Leader*, have opened their batteries already, and while the style of objection is different in the several prints, the objective point is the same in every case—the vast expense to the tax-payers attendant upon the passage of an ex-slave pension law. In some instances it has been asserted that it will entail upon the federal treasury a tax of two hundred billion dollars within the next thirty years! Could anything be more ridiculous? Why, estimating the number of slaves emancipated from bondage at five millions, and if all of them were alive to-day, and the government should pay into their hands a thousand dollars apiece, the total sum of the payment would only be five billion dollars, or one-fortieth of the sum it has been gravely stated the passage of the proposed pension law will entail upon the government in thirty years time ! As a fact, it may be said, the whole amount this pension act may call for will not amount to a tenth part of five billions.

But it is not the purpose of the writer to enter into an argument with the phantasy of a diseased or deluded brain. An appeal to logic and facts will be maintained in the face of derision. The enormous expense account attendant upon the passage of a just measure is not likely to frighten any person who desires to see the integrity of this great nation maintained in purity and reality. Had the people of the several states stopped to figure in 1861, when the shore batteries at Charleston were opened upon Fort Sumter, and had their cupidity exceeded their patriotism, it is probable there never would have been another shot fired after Major Robert Anderson and his gallant little band had made their surrender. But the expense attached to the maintenance of the war was not taken into account. Neither were the people appalled at a contemplation of the rivers of blood that must flow, the homes that must be made desolate, the dreary waste that must follow in the wake of contending armies, nor the millions that would be expended, year after year, for the pensions of union soldiers and their dependent families. After the lapse of nearly thirty years it is now found that the pension roll is many millions greater than it was when the angel of peace spread its wings over the land and put an estoppel upon the effusion of blood.

The questions to be decided are these: Was the act of emancipation right? Did the emancipation turn millions of slaves from homes of comfort into a condition of penury and want? Has the freedom of the negro entailed poverty upon the aged and helpless and made many of them the inmates of alms-houses and the subjects of public charity? If so, what is the plain duty of a great government to the helpless creatures whom it once rated as chattel property and compelled the taxation of their bodies for the support of the state?

These questions will have to be answered in the calmness of reason and not in the ribaldry of a cruel jest. Once presented fairly to the sober second thought of a justice-loving people, and the voice of humanity will speak to the hearts of the people, bidding them to do right at every hazard.

It has been already said that great reforms move slowly. But when they have once begun to move, there is no such thing as staying their onward march. When James G. Birney was first made the presidential candidate of the old liberty party in 1840, he received barely more than 7,000 votes in all the United States. He was a candidate again in 1844 and received 62,000 votes. The anti-slavery sentiment had begun to grow. Sixteen years later it swept the land, carrying down the old political organizations before it. It was persistent discussion that accomplished such a result. So will it be in the matter of righting the wrongs which our nation has suffered to exist. No ridicule, or denunciation, or effort to affright timid capital will be able to call a halt. The work in hand is right, and the right must and will prevail.

ADDRESS.

An open address to the Congressional Committee that now has, or that may hereafter have, the Ex-Slave Pension Bill before it for consideration, let me say:

GENTLEMEN OF THE COMMITTEE:—In asking consideration for the rough draft of an act, which I conceive to be just, having in view the pensioning of freedmen who have become old since they acquired their freedom in pursuance of the two proclamations of ex-President Lincoln and of the acts of congress and of the conventions of sovereign states whereby an enslaved people were made free, I have to say, that you will find much to be added and a wide range for an interchange of opinions as to the methods that ought to be observed in putting such an important work into successful operation. The principal thought involved is justice towards a once enslaved race, and to afford a people who have been made citizens and participants in the affairs of the government, with the means of competing with their fellow men of other races and better surroundings in the combat of life. As long as these people were regarded as chattels—the hewers of wood and the drawers of water for those who chanced to be placed above them in the circumstances of life—their physical comfort was looked after by those who received the direct benefit of their manual labor. But in the course of human events these men have been made free, and they have started in the race of life in competition with a race that has never suffered the horrors and injustice of subjugation. It may be apparent to you, gentlemen, that in such a race the negro suffers an unspeakable disadvantage. To expect that he

would be able to perform well the part assigned to him in his new
condition, is giving him credit for a superiority that does not
attach to human existence. It was honorable to the government
to accord him his freedom at a time when the life of the nation
appeared to tremble in the balance, but that he should have made
the very best use of freedom for the advancement of his own weal
and that of his late fellow slaves was scarcely to have been expected. The wonder is, that he has done as well for himself as
we observe him to have accomplished. Perhaps the white race,
similarly circumstanced, could not have done more.

You will admit, gentlemen, that the government did not make
the bondmen free from downright good will. It has been a boon
accorded to the down-trodden because in the sturdy forms and
physical strength of millions of slaves an element was seen that
might be made useful in the suppression of a gigantic rebellion.
It was manifestly the right and duty of those entrusted with the
administration of the government, to make use of those means
which God and nature had placed within their power. Even President Lincoln, at the outset of the rebellion, said that if he could
maintain the union by saving the institution of slavery, that he
would save it. But he found that the salvation of the union
depended largely upon the destruction of that institution, and he
struck the blow that surely destroyed it. Since then congress has
habilitated the freedmen with the right of franchise, and has opened
to him the avenues of preferment. What the Negro lacks is the
means placed in his hands that will enable him, and those that
come after him, to hold up their heads and take a part in the avocations of life that will be honorable and just to an enfranchised
race. This, gentlemen, congress can do by the passage of the bill
before you into a law, after your wisdom and experience shall have
perfected its details, and surrounded it with such safeguards as will
make it a prudent law for the colored citizens, while the federal
treasury will be sufficiently protected from fraud.

When the southern slaves were recognized as chattel property,
subject to all the fluctuations of an article that possessed a market-
able value, they were made the subjects of taxation, and as such
contributed their share of revenue to the treasury, in one shape
and another, enabling the government to declare war, conclude
peace and to contract alliances. After having been the subject of
taxation for the benefit of the government, that government has
seen fit to strike the shackles from the limbs of the slave and to
convert the chattel into a citizen. As a chattel, surrounded by an

implacable bondage, that could encompass no work but the service expected from vassalage, the negro could make no demand upon the government. Having been made a citizen without the asking of such a boon, it is the citizen that now arises and asks the government of which he is a part, to do by him that degree of justice that will enable him to perform an honorable part in life. Place in his hands the means to rival the white race and then judge him by the fruits of his afterwork. The bill before your committee, gentlemen, will go a long way in the direction of doing fairness and justice.

But there is another view of this question that is entitled to your candid consideration. Much of the prosperity that has attended northern communities since the conclusion of hostilities between the North and South, growing out of the late civil war, has come about in consequence of the quarterly distribution of pension money voted by congress to the surviving union soldiery. That source of prosperity has not extended to the southern states in a very large degree. Comparatively few union soldiers were enlisted at the South, and the number who have become residents of that section since the war make up but a light percentage of the general population. The passage of a measure that would place former slaves upon the pension rolls would not only be the performance of a delayed act of justice, to a once enslaved race, but it would occasion an expenditure of treasure throughout the entire southern region that would visibly enhance the material prosperity of all classes of people within that section. So it appears that every consideration of enlarged wisdom and political economy calls aloud for the passage of some such law as it is now your province to consider.

In conclusion, gentlemen, permit me to say that all great and generous nations have been ready and willing to make a valuable recompense for the wrongs they have perpetrated towards other nations or to individuals for errors of administration or acts of wrong or oppression. Indemnity between great states and growing out of a condition of war has been the rule of the world. Our own country exacted vast tribute from Mexico because of the war that raged in 1846 and 1847. The possession by us of California and the vast territories adjacent came to us in that way. France emptied into the coffers of Germany a nearly fabulous wealth in the settlement of their last appeal to arms. Great Britain did not hesitate to reimburse the people of this country with fifteen millions of money for the ravages committed upon American com-

merce during the existence of our civil war. But these things
were not a tithe of the error endured for ages by the enslaved
people of these states. We have sought in a measure to remedy
that error, but the remedy so far provided only exhibits to public
gaze the enormity of the wrong patiently endured, and for which
the pending measure provides more complete and ample satisfaction. As we measure justice to a wronged race of people so it may
be meted to us again should the hour of extremity ever come.

AN OPEN ADDRESS.

*To the colored citizens of the United States born in slavery and liber-
· ated by means of general emancipation :*

FELLOW CITIZENS : — Though not a member of Congress,
charged with the enactment of laws for the weal of all citizens of
our common country irrespective of race, class or condition, I am,
nevertheless, one who has given the subject of your emancipation
a candid study and considerable earnest thought, especially with
respect to the changes it has entailed upon you and your progeny,
and the just obligations which the government has assumed or
ought to have assumed in extending to your race the boon of
being made freemen. As one of the results of such thought and
investigation, I have prepared and had presented in Congress,
through the medium of my direct representative, a bill, which, in
my estimation, will make substantial progress in conferring upon
you the proper benefits of freedom and enable the younger
generation to perform well their part in the high field of
usefulness, wherein they have been made actors and participants.
I am not prepared to say that the bill in question covers all the
minutiæ of a comprehensive and intelligent law, but in general I
hope the benefits designed to be conferred are set forth with
such precision as to be comprehensible in respect to the intent and
purpose of the proposed act. Deficiencies can be readily supplied
and errors — if found to exist — can easily be remedied. The
main object in view will readily appear even to the most casual
observer, and I am persuaded that reflection and observation will
commend the measure to the approval of the sober second thought
of the people.

The general tenor of the bill presented to Congress and to the
people for the first time, comprehends the pensioning by the
government of such of the African race as were born in bondage

and have been made free by the Emancipation Proclamation of
Ex-President Lincoln and the laws of the United States and of the
several states of the Union where slavery formerly existed, organic
and statutory, which have been passed in pursuance of those
proclamations or consistently therewith. In shaping such a law
it has appeared just to me that a bonus in a suitable sum should
be given to those older persons who stood the brunt of years of
serfdom, and who in the order of nature have not long to remain
amongst us in the enjoyment of the blessings of freedom. This
bonus has been graduated in lesser sums to those recipients who are
younger in years and whose prospect of longer life it appears to
be natural to hope for, until a fair monthly stipend is only given
to those who did not suffer greatly the rigors of unjust laws and
who have the battle of life before them. As before stated, if
anything is wanting to make the operation of the proposed law
uniform and justly fair to the people sought to be benefited, that
want can easily be supplied when it is found to exist. For the
present a great work will have been done in case public attention
can be drawn to the subject in hand and a general approval of the
body politic secured.

It is proper for me to say that this subject is not a sudden
impulse on my part, and I have not thrust it before the law-
making power with undue haste. Many years have elapsed since
the inspiration of the righteousness of some such measure first
dawned upon my mind and since first I became persuaded that some
such proceeding was merited and due to a down-trodden people. I
have "made haste slowly" in bringing the subject to public
attention.   Like heroic old David Crockett I wished to " be sure I
was right and then go ahead."   To this end I have canvassed the
matter dispassionately with many leading and active citizens
— persons who were informed in public affairs — and have
corresponded with a great many others who occupy high stations
in civil life. With surprising uniformity I have found the subject
to be one that has been new to the people, generally requiring
thought and investigation to enable them to arrive at a conclusion
in the premises. In looking over my correspondence, which has
embraced experienced statesmen and law makers, I have not found
that any of them have been ready to advance a project that seems
to me just and equitable, and the performance of which ought not
to be longer seriously delayed. When President Harrison was in
the United States Senate I asked his opinion of the scheme now
laid before Congress, but did not obtain his thorough assent to the

proposition. Others like unto him were halting between two opinions. As years have rolled away since this matter was brought to their attention it is to be hoped that they are now ready to lend a helping hand in the promotion and success of a worthy cause. It may be that direful opposition will be meted out to the measure now brought to the notice of the people, but I am buoyed up in my purpose to have it thoroughly agitated by the reflection that all great reforms have triumphed over persistent opposition.

In addressing the colored people directly interested in the proposed measure, I wish to enlist them actively in a matter that appeals personally to them and theirs. Their correspondence and encouragement is solicited, and suggestions looking to the furtherance of the scheme, beneficial mainly to them, which is now for the first time publicly proposed, are most respectfully solicited.

I have prepared the following petition in order that all petitions signed might be alike, and have caused the same to be extensively published and circulated, and reproduce it here that you and all friends of justice may carefully read the same, and aid me at once in securing signers to Congress, that a great national wrong may be righted.

TO THE PRESS OF THE UNITED STATES.

Very recently the subscriber sent to all newspapers whereof he had knowledge, which make a specialty of representing the sentiments and feelings of the African race, either in business, religion or politics, copies of "The Omaha Sunday Democrat" containing the text of house bill 1,119, introduced in congress by Hon. W. J. Connell, of the First Nebraska district, at the request of W. R. Vaughan, proposing a pension for ex-slaves who were made free by the proclamation of Abraham Lincoln and subsequent acts of congress, the same being confirmed by constitutional amendments and statutory laws of the several states adopted at later dates. In most instances the newspaper organs of the colored people have been silent touching a measure of unquestionable justice to the subjects of slavery emancipation, probably through a becoming sense of modesty on the part of the managers and publishers.

Believing that the newspaper which appeals directly to negro support must have the interest of the race at heart, the subscriber makes no hesitation in asking such papers to spread before their readers a petition of the general form and sentiment:

To THE CONGRESS OF THE UNITED STATES: Believing that the men and women who were held in slavery prior to the war of the rebellion are entitled to just recompense for their years of involuntary servitude, the subscribers appeal to the congress of the United States for the passage of "Vaughan's Freedmen's Pension Bill," introduced in congress June 24, 1890, by the Hon. W. J. Connell, of Nebraska. The measure we conceive to be right in spirit, and it bears the evidence of true economy in its preparation. It recognizes the right of the claim of freedmen for aid, but it leaves them in a condition requiring industry in order that they may procure a comfortable and permanent maintenance. Therefore the subscribers beg leave to appeal to the humanity of congress in session in favor of the passage of the Vaughan Freedmen's Pension Bill.

Your petitioners will ever pray:

NAME	White	Colored	RESIDENCE	If a former slave, No. of years	Age	If a soldier, How long

Petitions similar to the above and other communications may be addressed to W. R. Vaughan, either at Omaha, Neb., or Washington, D. C., as he proposes to open an office in the latter city at an early day, and all communications addressed to Omaha will be forwarded there. Cut out the above petition and attach it to a sheet of legal cap paper, or re-write the substance of it if deemed best. The work taken in hand will be pursued to success or until death shall prevent further effort.

Will the representative press of the colored race and other newspapers friendly to a great cause kindly publish this circular as a matter of news and in justice to an oppressed people? It is believed that appropriate petitions, once fairly circulated, will be very largely signed. Address,

W. R. VAUGHAN, Omaha, Neb.,
Or Washington, D. C.

AFRICA.

Concluding an appeal to the congress, the states and the people, in behalf of the late subjects of slavery within the United States, it is just and fair to the subjects of a once enslaved race, to say to the readers of this volume, that it is a popular error which writes down the sons and daughters of Africa as barbarians from the beginning of time. They were not such, or all history is false in what it records of the human race. Speculation as to the correctness of the biblical version of the confusion of tongues and the separation of races, in the earliest ages of which we have any published account, would be vain. That the black race inhabited the continent of Africa is a point beyond dispute, but that they have always been ignorant, barbarous and brutal, is not sustained by any competent authority now extant. On the other hand the region of country lying north of the Great Desert is one of remote historical account, and it has been the seat of learning, science and vast mechanical skill. Egypt, and the country contiguous to the mouth of the Nile, has a history as old as civilization. But far back of any authenticated narrative of the present age, that country was peopled by a race of men cultured in the arts, sciences and useful mechanics, which are the rich heritages of a great, a powerful and a noble people. In the patriarchal ages Egypt was a land of corn and wine. When Western Asia was the seat of empire, where Abraham built the altar upon which to make a sacrifice of his son; where Jacob saw the ladder upon which angels were seen descending from heaven to earth, and returning to the regions of bliss again; where the brethren of Joseph sold him into captivity and sent him as a slave into Egypt, and by chance into the palace of the Phariohs; from whence the sons of Jacob journeyed to Egypt for bread, when Palestine was famishing with hunger, and there found the brother of the striped coat, installed in the palace of the king; in that ancient day Egypt was the land flowing with milk and honey, while the balance of the known world was a barren desert, where Gaunt Hunger was the monarch of all he surveyed.

Within the reign of the Phariohs, or following their control of empire, the Pyramids were built, and hecatombs were constructed, which have been the wonder of the world. Before the reign of the Caesars began at Rome, the seat of civilization was in upper Africa. There temples were built, monuments were raised, and wonders performed which have excited the admiration of the world during subsequent time. Who built the pyramids? What knowledge of mechanics did they possess by means of which solid stones, of the dimensions of 40,960 cubic feet, weighing 4,587,520 pounds, or nearly 2,300 tons, were elevated an hundred feet above the surface of the earth, and placed in a solid wall? Great men did this thing; and if we may believe the instruction of clearly convincing circumstances these men were Negroes!

Whatever may have been the blood of Cleopatra, whose arts led captive Mark Antony and defied the authority of the Cæsars, it cannot be questioned that she followed in the footsteps of the ancient Afric princes of Egypt. Although the black races of Northern Africa were driven across the desert and despoiled of their possessions, so did the power of the white race decline in Southern Europe, and the whole world was involved in darkness for many generations. It is not true that the Moors and other southern races of Europe were the progenitors of civilization in Egypt and the Barbary States. On the contrary, the Moors sprang from the expelled African races, driven out by internal dissentions of which there can be found no adequate account. The barbarism of the Negro rose from civil strife, fomented and encouraged by the grasping avarice of foreign powers.

As a grand division of the globe, Africa is the second in point of size, only being exceeded by Asia. It is known to current history, and will be for perhaps more than a century to come, as "the dark continent" and the land of mystery. During the nineteenth century a good deal has been done to open it up to us by the enterprise of explorers, the zeal of missionaries, the perseverance of commercial speculation and the military aggressions of dominant European powers. England, France and Germany are contending for the mastery, and the success of either of them means the gradual extirpation of the savage African nations which have been driven from their ancient seats of empire to become the tribal occupants of more southern regions and sea coast settlements south of Sahara. From the ranks of those refugees, as they become involved in turmoil, one community against another, the pirates from Europe have peopled the states of North and South America with slaves.

Even after the explorations of such learned prilgrims in the cause of discovery as Mungo Park, David Livingstone and Henry M. Stanley, Africa is comparatively an unknown region; but the more it is explored the more convincing becomes the settled conclusion that its native population has grown up from scattered fragments of colonies driven out of the northern region by the dread circumstance of war. The extent of its population is unknown. Some travelers and writers have estimated the native inhabitants to be as low as twenty-five millions of people, while others have stated one hundred millions to be too low a figure. All agree, however, that the progress of degradation has gradually gone forward since the days when the ancient population was driven away from home and possessions to become a race of wanderers upon the earth. In their first settlement, even in the wilderness, some of the pioneers carried with them a knowledge of mechanic arts and processes which have gradually been lost as the cloud of ignorance and superstition settled over the people. They built cities, the ruins of which have been found. They had great and elaborate works of art, and were successful as agriculturalists. There are yet to be found evidences of ancient religious training, showing that the races sprang from a parentage which believed in One Source and Supremacy of Eternal Power. But, as contact with the world was forgotten, barbarism became the rule; and in place of an abode of learning and useful arts, "the dark continent" has supplied the world with the most lamentable examples of human misery and the most hideous instances of crime. As a strong community prayed upon a weak, and men and women were constantly made captives in war, even the savage heart became sated with rapine and butchery; and their reduction of captives to a condition of slavery followed just as naturally as the darkness of night follows the light of day.

The spoliation of ordinary robbers and buccaneers did not complete the work of African subjugation, the extension of primal slave-making having been the work of Christian nations, which carried the captives of robber chieftains into foreign lands. There the captive of the savage became the slave of the bible reading people, who daily blessed God because the creatures of bondage had fallen into the hands of pious people able to learn them the straight and narrow path that leads to the throne of heaven!

It has been truly remarked of Africa that the dark continent presents the singular anomoly of having been the home of ancient civilization, and the prey of the modern rapacity and plunder of all nations. It is natural, therefore, that in regard to the plundered portions of this vast area the world should be comparatively uninformed, even after the explorations of the last half century, which have given a wider knowledge of its physical geography and of the character of its savage inhabitancy than had hitherto been possessed.

As long ago as the fifteenth century explorers from Portugal made tours of examination and discovery along the east and west coasts of Africa. In that day Portugal was perhaps the first maritime power in Europe. The crown gave kingly encouragement to tours of discovery. These were prosecuted not only along the shores of Africa, in the eastern hemisphere, but extensively in the western hemisphere, with respect to North and South America and the West India islands, following the first discoveries of Columbus. This spirit of adventure gave to Portuguese merchants the advantage of learning the source of supplying vessels with slaves in Africa, and also of knowing a ready and valuable market in the new world. But while engaged in their explorations the Portuguese made valuable discoveries, which are of consequence in showing that many of the African tribes had maintained a fair order of civilization in spite of their forcible expulsion from their ancient realm into the savagery of the wilds lying south of the equator. Vasco de Gama made a voyage as early as 1497 which resulted in the discovery of Natal, Mozambique and a number of small islands off the coast of Africa, and in them he found a people which enjoyed a high state of commercial advancement and very many of the evidences of civilization which had come to them from the reign of Cleopatra and the time wherein the Cæsars ruled Egypt. With their banishment they had not degenerated into a savage state, but had maintained a fair degree of the eminent condition which pervaded Northern Africa in the palmy days of the splendor and refinement of their forefathers. True, they had fallen under the influence of the missionaries of Mohammed and adopted the faith of the prophet of Allah. But this fact is not surprising when it is remembered that the birthplace of Jesus Christ has become abject in its acknowledgment of Mohammedan rule, while Jerusalem, the city of the Great King, has a Mosque on the sacred spot where the Savior once expelled harpies and traders from the temple, declaring to them that they had made the Father's house a den of thieves. All over the land where the Man of Sorrows pursued his earthly ministry, and wrought his miracles, the prevailing religion to-day is that of Mohammed. No wonder, then, that the followers of the Prophet had extended their proselytism to the islands lying along the African coast, prior to the time when Vasco de Gama came among them with vessels from Portugal having the wings of the sea.

De Gama found, in the islands which he visited, a population enjoying all the elegant advantages of well-built cities, ports, mosques for the worship of Allah according to the teachings of the Moslem faith, and carrying on a valuable trade with India and the Spice Islands by means of rude boats propelled partly with oars and partly with sails of native manufacture. Vessels from Portugal regularly visited this region for a long series of years after the discovery of De Gama, and Portuguese merchants secured an affluent trade. In the meantime the news of the discovery went abroad, and other European powers established colonies at different places on the African coast; so that in the sixteenth century a general examination of the coast line of Africa was made from the mouth of the River Senegal, on the west coast, to the entrance into the Gulf of Aden on the east coast, being the south entrance into the waters of the Red Sea.

Notwithstanding these advances in matters of African exploration nearly two hundred years passed away before enterprising efforts were made to penetrate the interior of the continent. All that had been done amounted to a geographical and mercantile exploration of the coast line and the establishment of a few commercial settlements. The English government effected a settlement at the Cape of Good Hope, and with characteristic enterprise occupied the territory immediately tributary to their colony. From this base of operations that government has spread out its work of aggrandizement until it now controls the bulk of the African trade. But in all that the agents of the British nationality have discovered, there has been no fact brought to light which will gainsay the theory that the Negro races of Africa, however barbarized or unlettered, have not been the descendants of a civilized condition of society at some remote era. Those tribes which have been most oppressed, and made the subjects of incursions by more powerful bands, in the interests of slave traders, have sunk deepest into degradation. It is those which have been able to maintain a well regulated system of defense, and to keep at bay predatory incursionists, that present to strangers who have visited them the evidences of natural superiority and the unmistakable indications of having known a better day.

It was not until 1795 that Mungo Park, an adventursome Scotch explorer, who had conceived the idea of breaking the shell of outer Africa, and penetrating the interior, with a view of learning what might be found there, proceeded to put his enterprise into operation. After two years of hardship and privation he returned to Great Britain and published a volume recounting his discoveries and hair-breadth escapes, which, for a time, were the marvels of the world, surpassing the captivating stories of fiction. His narrative was reduced to entertaining simplicity, published partially in school books, and in small volumes for the attraction of youth. But the point with which we mainly have to deal is the fact that he found the Mohammedan religion prevailing along the banks of the Niger, carrying out the idea that even the barbarous tribes furnished evidence of having descended from a higher plane of life. Mungo Park made a second voyage to Africa in 1805, and lost his life by drowning on the upper waters of the Niger, where he was ambushed by natives in a narrow pass, and sought to escape by swimming to the opposite shore.

The observations of Mungo Park and the discoveries made by him whetted the desire for further information. Denham and Clapperton, English merchants, in 1822, fitted out a caravan from Tripoli, on the Mediterranean sea, from whence the expedition crossed the Great Desert and reached Lake Tchad, on the line dividing the districts of Kanem and Bornu, in interior Africa, from which point an extensive exploration of contiguous territory was made. This expedition confirmed many of the theories of Mungo Park in the conclusion that South Africa had once been a seat of great enterprise, accompanied with a fair degree of civilization.

With the later discoveries of Dr. David Livingstone, and, following him, of the intrepid American adventurer, Henry M. Stanley, the reading people of the whole world are fully familiar. While the people of almost every land on the globe are perusing the last narrative of Stanley, it is unnecessary to repeat the conditions which he has found to exist. He has imparted sufficient information for cultured men to arrive at the just conclusion that Africa has not always been the dark continent as it now appears to us, but that it has been the theater of great exploits in the past ages, the record of which has been lost to mankind.

This line of thought and deduction has been pursued by the writer with a view of convincing men of the white race, who may take time to peruse this volume, that the Negro race is capable of the highest degree of civilization, and that the dusky people of African abstraction can maintain a place with honor along side of the most famous nations of the globe. All that is required to prove the force and truth of such a theory is to give the Negro a fair start in life as a newly made freeman; and in no way can this work be more speedily and satisfactorily accomplished than by giving an adequate compensation to those of the race who have been unjustly held in vassalage from their youth up. While righting a wrong the men and women who have suffered wrong will be started upon a new existence. They will hold up their heads in pride, because the country they love and have served, both in bondage and as freemen, has had the courage to do them justice.

It would be manifestly unjust to the Negro people of America for this discussion of what Africa has been in the past, to be closed without calling attention to a criticism which has been often indulged, even by men holding high places in the government.

The objection has been raised against the Negro, as a distinctive feature of the human race, that his subjugation and reduction to a condition of slavery constituted an unanswerable argument against his capacity of maintaining a high standard of excellence after having arrived at such an eminence. Surely this view has not been well taken, and facts certainly will not support it. Because Africa has been the seat of learning and empire, and has been peopled by a race who builded cities and towns and monuments of greatness, and, after the lapse of ages, her population became dispersed, her knowledge of learning destroyed and the genius of her great inventors brought to nought, it cannot be said that other people of various races have not suffered the same degradation and humiliation. The researches which have been made upon American soil teaches the unmistakable lesson that in this land there once existed a nation, or nations, taught in the highest degree of scholastic information. The buried cities which have been brought to light tell the story of lost greatness in terms that cannot be misunderstood.

Beginning with the researches of John L. Stephens in Central America, and adding to the information which he imparted to the world the subsequent discoveries of other explorers, we must admit that the North American continent was peopled, in a forgotten past, by races of men who were skilled in all the arts and sciences requisite to make enlightened nations. They builded cities, raised temples and monuments and conducted a thriving commerce, of which convincing traces have been found.

Who were these people? Whence did they come? How were they overthrown? Was it by the arms and prowess of conquerors, or by some terrible commotion of nature? If the former, what became of the conquerors? If the latter, may it not be equally true that the learning, the greatness and the productive wealth of ancient African nations fell before the hurricane, the whirlwind or the earthquake of nature, just as American cities were buried and wiped out of existence?

When Christopher Columbus discovered the western hemisphere, he found here tribes of savages of a lineage before unknown to the world. As subsequent discoveries were made in new quarters there continued to be found tribes differing in some features, but preserving the general outlines of one people. Whether these tribes descended from an ancient population which dwelt in cities and pursued avocations of civilized life, cannot be known. All is a matter of conjecture and speculation. But the fact remains that the work of destruction once swept over the land wherein we live, just as it did over the continent of Africa. Whether the besom of destruction was simultaneous in both hemispheres, or whether countless ages intervened between the visitation of wrath in the two lands, is a problem which may never be solved. But the conclusion is irresistible that the Negro race is no more accountable for the destruction which visited Africa, than that the races found on American soil can be held responsible for the overturning of the empire which once flourished here.

In her day Babylon was a great city, the home of prophets and patriarchs, the seat of learning, luxury and fabulous wealth. Her rulers were the most powerful men of earth. The glory of the great city was the wonder of the world, and her splendor appeared likely to endure forever. That city fell, and the site where it existed is the abode of the howling hyena and other savage beasts of the forest. The Negroes who dwelt in the buried cities of Africa should not be regarded as careless defenders of their pristine glory any more than that the Asiatic natives should be gibbeted for having suffered Babylon to fall.

The duty of the men of the present day is to discard all cavil, and to face manfully the stubborn fact that the government of the United States did, for three-quarters of a century, suffer a gigantic wrong to be perpetrated upon an enslaved race. The stigma of that wrong will endure forever, unless the government shall recompense the survivors of the race who patiently endured such a flagrant act of injustice. The performance of an act of justice owing to the ex-slaves of the United States, will redound to the honor of a great nation and will receive the admiration and encomium of all the generous and noble people of the world.

.